ONLY THE LIES

AN 'ONLY YOU' SERIES STANDALONE

ELLE THORPE

WWW.ELLETHORPE.COM

For Thomas.
After years of watching Taekwondo practices, it had to feature in a book at some point! I'm proud of you, my little provisional black belt!

BLURB

Him: Six foot, four inches. Thor look-alike. Kickass black belt ninja man, and gym owner.

Me: Barely five foot. Resembles an overstuffed dumpling. Semi-decent receptionist of the office across the road.

Match made in heaven? I think so. Which is why I get to work early each morning, and stare longingly out the window, desperate for my daily glimpse of him.

The man doesn't know I'm alive, and I don't have the lady balls to do anything about it. Until the postman delivers the gym's mail to my office. It's the perfect excuse to strut over there and introduce myself, right?

Wrong.

When he mistakes me for someone else, I'm so blinded by his abs that I don't correct him. And now he's calling me someone else's name, and I don't know how to turn this around apart from to bolt back to my desk with my ass jiggling behind me.

I never expected he'd follow me.

Or anything that happened next.

Only the Lies is a standalone in the Only You series. If you love it, the boxset is on sale and only $5.99 during January and February 2021! That's over $10 off the regular price of all five books. Or download it FREE in Kindle Unlimited! Download here.

1

The clinic door banged open. "Did I miss him?" Bree panted, staggering over to join me at the window.

I shook my head. "Not yet. Should be any minute now."

We both peered through the slatted blinds like the stalkers we were, neither of us bothering to acknowledge Damien, my boss and Bree's boyfriend, when he struggled through the door a minute later, juggling coffee and breakfast for the three of us.

He dumped his armful of takeaway bags and trays on the reception desk, then leaned back on it, picking up the pile of mail I'd left there.

"Bree," he said casually, "you do remember that I'm your boyfriend, right? I'm nice. Funny. Somewhat attractive? A lesser man would be devastated by your actions, you know."

Bree looked over her shoulder and blew him a kiss. "You know you're my number one, babe. But this guy..."

"Yeah, yeah, I know. Buns of steel."

I dragged my gaze away from the parking lot, that was still irritatingly empty of one oversized black ute and the oversized man that drove it. "Buns of steel? Really? You think that's why we stare out the window each morning, waiting for him to drive in? It has nothing to do with that."

He snorted. "Oh, really?"

I grinned. "Nope, it has more to do with the biceps, and the abs—"

"The man has a shirt on every morning, Cleo. How have you seen his abs?"

"Oh, we've seen them, all right," Bree confirmed. "You can see them through his shirt. *That's* how cut he is. And there was that one time..."

I let my head drop back on my shoulders and made prayer hands while I thanked the big guy upstairs. "The day he *ran* to work with no shirt on. That blessed day where the heavens opened and birds sang and—"

"Hey!" Bree squealed, as Damien covered her eyes and dragged her away from the window. "I'm going to miss the show."

"How bout I give you a show of my own?"

"Oh, really?"

"Mmmm hmmm."

Damien's lips brushed Bree's neck, and suddenly Bree was more interested in her man than being my wing-woman. I groaned good-naturedly when Damien dragged her back toward his office and closed the door.

"Patients will be here in thirty, Damien! I'm not covering for you!"

"Move my first appointment," he yelled through the closed door. "I'm gonna need at least an hour."

Bree's laughter echoed back.

He was joking. He and Bree were still in the honeymoon phase, and were somewhat sickening in the way they fawned over each other. I didn't doubt for a second that they'd gotten it on in that office at some point. As the head doctor of the practice, he could take some leniencies. But Damien was a pro when he needed to be. I hadn't had to move any of his appointments yet. And Bree had class at nine, so she'd be leaving in the next five minutes anyway.

Which gave me five more minutes to stare out this window until my morning dose of eye candy arrived.

A flash of black caught my eye at the driveway we shared with the handful of other buildings in the complex. My breath stuttered and my stomach did a little flip-flop.

He was here.

His ute rolled into his designated parking spot in front of the rundown gym, and he swung his long legs out. My gaze rolled up his athletic body. Blue sneakers today. Black gym shorts that showed off tanned, muscular calves. A sleeveless singlet shirt with the gym's logo printed on the back left his biceps exposed, and I watched in fascination as his muscles moved beneath his skin. He slammed the ute's door shut and, all too quickly, disappeared behind the tinted glass windows of the building.

I let out a breath laced with disappointment. Well, that was the best part of my day over. Once the practice opened, I was always too busy at my desk, organising patients or Damien, to do any more window-stalking. And that was probably a good thing. It was bad enough that I got to work early every morning just to feed my ridiculous crush. The only thing that would come from me having more time to perv on him would be a restraining order.

The lovebirds tumbled back into the waiting room, and Bree nudged me with her elbow as she made her way to the door. "Singlet or shirt today?"

A wide grin spread across my face. "Singlet."

She clutched her heart and groaned dramatically. "See what you made me miss?" she called to Damien and he shook his head, not bothering to look up from the pile of mail he'd resumed sorting.

A secretive smirk lifted the corner of his mouth. "You weren't complaining a minute ago."

Bree gave me a wink, and I rolled my eyes.

"Cleo, for the sake of my relationship, will you please just ask the man out?" Damien complained.

My skin broke out in a cold sweat. "Uh, no. Not a chance in hell."

Bree stuck her hands on her hips like a pouty toddler. "But why?"

Because the man had to have a girlfriend. Or worse, a wife. Because he looked like a supermodel while I looked like a short, overweight dumpling. Bree wouldn't understand any of those things. She was tall and had legs up to her ears. No man in his right mind would turn her down.

Plus there was one more huge barrier standing between me and the gym god running off into the sunset together. Bree didn't know my family. Or that all hell would break loose if they knew how I was pathetically pining after a guy who

owned a martial arts training gym.

"Well, looks like it's my lucky day." Damien waved an envelope around in the air, saving me from answering Bree. We both turned to look at him. "We got some of the gym's mail. I guess I'll just go over there and—"

"I'll do it!" Bree and I both yelled.

"Bree!" Damien and I said in unison.

She lowered her hand and turned pink. "Cleo will do it. Is what I meant," she said sheepishly.

Damien handed me the envelope, then turned back to Bree and whispered in her ear. "You'll pay for that one. Tonight. Heels only."

I covered my ears. "Ugh, Damien! Work on your whispering," I groaned. "Excuse me while I go vomit somewhere at that thought. I'll deliver this while I'm at it."

"Have fun!" Bree called.

"Don't wait up," I joked, throwing them both an exaggerated wink. I left them to their ribbing, only the teeniest bit jealous of their relationship. You knew things were solid between a couple when one could openly check out the hot guy across the street and the other just rolled their eyes.

I wanted that. I wanted to get to that place in a relationship where I was comfortable enough to be myself. To goof around and make jokes and tease. To have someone tell me to be wearing nothing but heels tonight. The best I'd done in years was a handful of lousy Tinder dates with creeps who did some serious photoshopping on their profile pics.

I followed the pedestrian path that ran around the edges of the parking lot, and tossed my hair back off my shoulders, trying to strut confidently. For a brief moment, I let my brain wander into a fantasy land where gym hottie watched me through the window the same way I watched him. He'd lock the door of the gym behind me, flip the closed sign, then bend me over the reception desk—no wait, that wouldn't work, because for one, glass windows, even if they were tinted, were see-through. And two, if I was ever getting down and dirty with this guy, I wanted to be facing him.

Running my hands up those biceps I admired every morning.

Pulling his sweat-soaked shirt off, and trailing my fingers down his abs and beneath his—

Woah. My face had gone hot, and I had to stop for a moment, my hand resting on the cool handle of the gym door. *Get a grip, Cleo. The man doesn't know you're alive. And if he did, he probably wouldn't appreciate you mentally undressing him.*

My hand shook, but I pushed open the door, a blast of cool

air smacking me in the face. I tried to force my smile to look natural while butterflies rioted in my belly. I was actually going to talk to him.

This was my moment.

Once Bree had found out about my mammoth crush, we'd come up with a whole list of ways for me to meet him, but they'd always seemed so forced and fake. I'd been happy to bide my time and wait for the perfect, non-forced moment. And this was it. I had an honest-to-God reason to be here and to introduce myself to him. Despite Bree and Damien's encouragement to just ask the man out, I knew I was never going to do that. But I wanted to know his name. Maybe if I knew his name, I could raise a hand in greeting if we ever happened to be in the parking lot at the same time. Or if we ran into each other at the grocery store. That had happened twice now, and he'd walked straight by me, without a hint of recognition. If I knew his name, he'd know mine.

But as I looked around the large room, there wasn't a person in sight. Definitely no tall, broad-shouldered object of my dreams. It was quiet. Much quieter than the gyms I'd been in. The reception desk was to the right, but no one stood behind it. No phones rang, no printers buzzed. A small waiting or perhaps meeting area sat to the left. Old leather armchairs were arranged around a coffee table with a few fitness magazines on top. I sniffed, but the air didn't smell of sweat like I'd semi expected it to. A clean, lightly perfumed scent lingered instead.

The rhythmic thumping of someone pounding a boxing bag suddenly filtered back, and I tightened my fingers around the envelope in my hand. I could just leave it on the reception desk and go back to work. That would be the smart thing to do. That's what a normal woman in her thirties who wasn't completely hard up and somewhat starving for male attention would do.

But let's face it. I was not that woman.

So I wandered around a corner, my mouth drying as he came into view. All six foot four of rippling muscle, pounding the crap out of a boxing bag. He roundhouse kicked it, his execution perfect, and I made a mental note to apologise to Damien because the man did have buns of steel. Buns I'd like to take a bite out of—

"Can I help you?"

Oh shit. He'd seen me.

I opened my mouth to answer, but no words came out. Up close, he was even more of an Adonis than I'd first thought. Even though we were still several feet apart, I had to look up to take in his face. His light-coloured hair was buzzed close to his scalp. Light-coloured eyes. Blue? No, green. The perfect-length beard. More than stubble but not long. Just how I liked it.

Shit. Had I spoken yet? I should speak. That's what people did when someone asks a question.

"Mrs Clour?" he tried again.

I found myself nodding.

Wait, why the hell was I nodding? That wasn't my name! Cleo Clour would have been a cruel and unusual punishment by my parents. But oh. He was smiling and coming toward me. Wow. His teeth were perfectly white and perfectly straight. Of course, they were. As if this man would have crooked chompers.

"Sorry I wasn't out the front. I wasn't expecting you until nine, but that's fine. We can do the tour now."

The tour? What tour? Tell him you made a mistake, Cleo. Tell him you don't know your own name when he's around but that you just came to drop off mail...

Yeah, that so wasn't happening. I looked at my watch in a panic. Quarter to nine. The real Mrs Clour wouldn't be here until nine. I could follow him around the gym for fifteen minutes, then scoot back to my desk across the parking lot, all in time to avoid revealing that I wasn't who he thought I was.

And hopefully in time to avoid being fired from my job.

"Mrs Clour?"

I gave him a lopsided smile. "You can call me Cleo."

"Cleo. Nice name."

Oh holy shit. The way my name rolled off his tongue. I had to give my knees a stern, internal lecture about keeping me standing. Melting to a puddle at his feet would probably not be a good look.

"Thanks. What's yours?"

"Oh, right. Sorry." He stuck his hand out. "I'm Beau. I'm the owner."

Beau. Yep. That fit. Sexy name for a sexy man. I stared at his big hand for a moment. Imagining those strong fingers travelling over my body...

Beau gave me a strange look, and I quickly grasped his hand between mine. Strong. Warm. Definitely skilled. I bet he knew exactly how to make a woman come undone with those fingers.

Beau coughed a little, and I realised I'd been holding his hand too long. Shit! Blood rushed to my face. *Good work, Cleo, you're doing great at hiding the fact that you're mildly in love with him. Should have just spray-painted it on your forehead. That would have been less subtle.*

I dropped his hand like it was hot, and he motioned for me to follow him through the gym.

"Like I told you on the phone, we mostly focus on martial arts training classes. We have boxing, Taekwondo, kickboxing, and mixed classes. But there's a weights area just over there. And cardio equipment on your left. You said you were interested in classes, though?"

I nodded. "Sure." I nearly choked on the lie. I hated gyms. And I hated martial arts. Once upon a time, I'd spent a lot of time in facilities that looked just like these. But now I avoided them like the plague. Which was why I'd never come over here pretending I was thinking of joining. That had been Bree's first suggestion when we'd made our "Ways to Meet the Hot Gym Guy" list. But I just couldn't do it. He would know instantly I wasn't a gym goer.

I was hardly what anyone would call petite. Curvy was probably a nice way of putting that I was at least ten kilos overweight. I'd started putting on weight years ago when I'd first stopped training. And it had snowballed from there. It wasn't so much the weight that bothered me. It was just how unfit I'd become. But gyms and I were over.

"We offer massage and some sports physiotherapy too. Some of the guys who train here are pretty into the higher levels so we try to accommodate them as well as the regular gym goer."

"Sounds great. Nice place you have."

Beau gave me a sharp glance, and I wondered if he thought I was being sarcastic. It probably had been a bad choice of words. The place wasn't nice. It was old and rundown, and the equipment looked outdated. But you didn't need a lot of fancy equipment to teach martial arts. It actually looked like a pretty appealing place for a beginner who didn't want a ton of people watching while she embarrassed herself. I was sure the real Mrs Clour would be very happy working out there, especially if Beau was around.

If things had been different, I might have been tempted to sign up myself.

We'd circled the whole facility, which really wasn't very big, and come back to the waiting area. "So, that's the grand tour," he said, his voice low and gruff.

So sexy.

My gaze wandered over his face—his strong jawline and the fine lines around his eyes that told me he was maybe older than I'd thought. He seemed to be studying me too. I lost myself a little in those green eyes, then realised he hadn't said anything for longer than normal. He was waiting on a response from me, but I hadn't heard a word he'd said. My cheeks went hot.

"Sorry, what was that?"

"Coffee?"

"I'd love to," I blurted out. But then I heard myself. Oh no. Wrong words! Wrong words!

He looked at me strangely. "Have a seat. I'll just grab you one."

He hadn't meant it as a date. Of course not. That was ridiculous. Even if the man was remotely attracted to me, he thought I was the *married* Mrs Clour. And if I knew anything about Beau, I knew he was a good, upstanding sort of man. Not that I actually did know anything about Beau. But the person he was in my head, the one I dreamed about, would never go after a married woman.

Beau walked away and I sunk down into the armchair. What the hell was I doing? Besides making a complete fool of myself. I had definitely reached certifiably crazy levels. There was a psychologist just a few doors down. I'd book myself an appointment on the way back to work.

It would be the sanest thing I'd done all morning.

I put the envelope down on the coffee table and was tiptoeing to the door when it swung open and a blonde woman in active wear strutted in, forcing me back. There was no bravado in the way she walked. She was tall and toned and moved like a panther. From the look of her abs, *she* was no stranger to the gym. I wrapped my arms around my roly middle and tried to slip out the door.

"Mrs Clour?" Beau called.

"Yes," the woman and I both answered. My stomach sunk. Somewhere between following around the buns of steel and getting a little lost in his green eyes, I'd managed to forget the woman whose identity I'd conveniently stolen was going to turn up at any minute. Damn it! I was the worst criminal ever.

Beau looked between the woman and I. But the real Mrs Clour beat me to the punchline. "I'm Hayley Clour. Here for the gym tour? I spoke to someone on the phone."

Beau's eyebrows drew together in confusion.

Where was a man-eating sinkhole when you needed one? Because I sure needed one.

Blondie was saying something to him, completely ignoring the fact that I was even in the room, and I took the opportunity to push my way out the door and hurry back toward the clinic. It was either leave with my tail between my legs or die of embarrassment right there at his feet.

"Wait, hold on a second!" Beau's gravelly voice came from behind me, and my eyes widened. Why was he coming after me? Go back to Mrs Fitness!

I increased my pace and ran as fast as my short, chubby legs would carry me. Oh my God. I was actually *running* away. Who even knew I could run anymore? It had been years since I'd tried. I tried to ignore my ass jiggling around, and the fact that he could likely see that through my work skirt. He caught up easily and jogged along beside me until I realised exactly how ridiculous this whole thing was and skidded to a stop.

I looked up at him sheepishly.

"Who are you?"

I grimaced. "Cleo. That bit was true. I work at the gynaecology practice. That one just over there. The doctor there is great if you ever need a gyn..."

I shut my mouth and closed my eyes. *Stop talking, Cleo. Just stop.* The poor man looked completely baffled by my behaviour. I couldn't blame him. *I* was completely baffled by my behaviour. I'd never had much chill, but the last twenty minutes had really taken the cake.

"So you just...what? Wasted my time letting me show you around the gym? Why? Were you ever planning on joining?"

I shook my head. "No," I admitted. "I hate gyms. I brought your mail."

Beau squinted at me like I wasn't making any sense.

"Okay, well, I'm going to go now before the men in white coats come to take me away. It was nice to meet you, Beau...sorry about, well, everything since I walked in the door."

I took a few steps backwards, trying to ignore how adorable he was when he was confused, and then turned and fled to the safety of my office.

"How'd it go?" Damien asked as I crashed through the door and took cover behind the reception desk. I slunk down onto the floor by his shoes and covered my face with my hands.

I could hear his stifled laugh, and it only made my face burn hotter.

"That good, huh?"

I nodded. That good.

2

_____

"Hey, Poly is here!" my dad yelled across the yard when I rocked up at his place on Sunday afternoon. I smiled brightly at him, but on the inside, I grimaced at the use of the childhood nickname I hated so much. My dad dropped a kiss on my hair, then went back to prodding the steaks he had on the BBQ.

My brothers, gathered around the outdoor table, barely looked up. Luca mumbled a hello, but the four of them were engrossed in a video playing on Dylan's phone. Ah the joys of being the baby sister in a house full of men. I was never particularly interesting to them if there was sports, beer, or food around.

"Ooooh!" Jesse yelled, thumping Spencer on the back. "You got your ass handed to you."

Spencer elbowed him in the ribs, hard enough that Jesse grunted and clutched his side. "I didn't show you so you could fucking laugh, you dickwad. I showed you so you'll help me at training tomorrow."

I flicked the top off a beer bottle I'd fished out of a cooler and settled in beside Luca. "What are you guys watching?" I asked.

Though I could guess. Same thing they were always watching. Doing. Thinking about.

"Spencer's fight from last night."

I nodded and took a sip of my beer. That explained the black eye Spencer was sporting. Though black eyes were so common with my brothers that I never even commented on them anymore. The four of them fell back into conversation about the upcoming week's training schedule and I zoned out. After a while, I wandered into the kitchen and pulled some salad vegetables from the crisper of the fridge.

I don't know how many times I'd told them that I didn't particularly love just eating a hunk of meat every time I came for dinner. A side salad or a soup starter wouldn't kill them, surely? I don't know why I kept expecting anything different though. It had been exactly the same growing up here. Which is why I'd left the minute I turned sixteen and could get a full-time job. Once upon a time I would have been right in the middle of it all with my brothers. But now, there was too much testosterone in this house. It was stifling.

I carried my salad out to the backyard table, knowing full well I'd be the only one to eat it. My brothers had already grabbed their plates of dead cow from the BBQ and were busy covering the meat in sauce. I put my salad bowl down, then took a plate for myself. They'd left me two slightly charred sausages. Good of them.

"So how's work, Cleo?" Jesse finally asked, pushing a lock of russet-coloured hair out of his eyes. Dylan looked up at me in surprise, making me wonder if he'd even realised I'd arrived.

"Fine."

"Gone on any hot dates lately?" Luca asked with a wide-mouthed grin.

I glared at him. Why did they always have to ask that? Just

because he slept around like a professional panty-dropper. "You used to be my favourite, you know?"

He pulled a face. "What did I say?"

I sighed. "Nothing. No. No dates."

"You need any money, Poly?" Dad asked.

"Why? You want to buy me a man, Pop?"

Luca guffawed and I knew I should take back the comment. It wasn't fair. Offering me money every time he saw me was Dad's way of caring, but it had always grated on my nerves. I had a job. It might not pay as much as he and my brothers earned, but it was a respectable living and I always paid my bills on time. Plus, the use of "Poly" twice in such a short space of time made me want to punch something. Or someone. One of my asshat brothers probably.

"You'll find a good man one of these days. You don't need to buy one."

I nodded my head slowly. "Thanks, Dad. Sorry. I'm in a mood. Just ignore me." He meant well. He really had no idea how to talk to me, that was all. None of them did. Not since I'd stopped blindly following in their footsteps. Most of the time, I was okay with the decisions I'd made. But there was no doubt, those decisions had made me the outsider in my own family. And that hurt. A family BBQ, on top of the beating my ego had already taken with Beau on Friday, was enough to make even a saint testy.

For the next hour, it was more of the same—shop talk dominating the conversation. Together, the five of them ran a chain of fitness clubs my father had started when we were kids. TAS Sports and Fitness. The clubs all had a heavy focus on a variety of martial arts disciplines as that was the current "in" thing. But my family's drug of choice was Taekwondo. We'd all been out on the mats before we could even walk, never given a choice in whether we actually wanted to learn or not.

I was the only one who had gone against the grain and given it up. Teenage rebellion and all that. That's what my father had put it down to, when at fifteen, I'd refused to keep training. I'd let him think that was all it was.

The boys got distracted by shop talk, and thankfully, that was the end of the love-life grilling. Eventually, I pulled my Kindle out of my bag just so I didn't have to hear them list out the virtues of Schneider vs O'Malley head guards. I'd learned to come prepared to these dinners. My brothers all had one-track minds and the conversation rarely skewed from sports or the gym. It was what it was. They were my family and I loved them. I wanted to see them, but we just had nothing in common.

When I'd had enough of reading, I carried the dirty plates to the kitchen and loaded the dishwasher. I found my bag on the dining room table and stuck my head out the door to say good-bye. I'd come for dinner, like I'd been asked. I'd hung around for a while. And now I could go home, guilt-free, feeling like a dutiful daughter.

"Man, I am so stoked for Bali. Did you guys get the email I sent? Did you see the view from our cabin?" Jesse asked.

"I saw," Dad answered.

I paused in my exit strategy.

"I'm going to own that mountain," Luca threw in. "I've already started reorganising the roster at work so we can all be off at the same time. I really need to get some more casuals in, though."

"What are you talking about?" I asked.

Five sets of eyes all turned to me. But for the longest time, no one said anything.

"What?"

"Ah, Cleo. We didn't realise you were still here," my Dad eventually said.

As insulting as that was, it wasn't unusual. "Are you all going somewhere?"

Dylan and Spencer both looked away. Luca blushed pink.

My eyebrows drew together. Cowards. There was something they didn't want to tell me. And it seemed they were all willing to lump it on our eldest brother to fill me in.

"Jesse?"

"Uh, yeah. We booked a trip."

"A work thing?" While I couldn't remember a time they'd ever *all* needed to go somewhere for work, it wouldn't be completely out of the question.

Jesse glanced around at our brothers awkwardly, but none of them were helping him out. I folded my arms across my chest. They all looked guilty as sin.

"Dad?"

He sighed. "Honey, you wouldn't enjoy it. That's the only reason we didn't invite you."

"Wouldn't enjoy what?"

The silence was deafening.

Realisation dawned on me. "You planned a *family* holiday and didn't invite me." Despite the fact that I'd just sat through hours of them ignoring me, the knowledge sat like a stone in my gut. At least I'd been invited to dinner. I hadn't even warranted an invitation to a holiday they were *all* going on? "I'm right, aren't I?" I said dully.

"It's not exactly a holiday," Luca piped up. "It's hiking and climbing, and you just wouldn't..."

"Wouldn't what, asshole? Wouldn't like to be invited to spend time with my family? Wouldn't like, for just one time, if you guys thought to include me in some of your plans?"

"We just didn't think you'd want to come, Cleo," Dad said in an annoyingly patronising voice. "It's not a lounge-on-the-beach sort of holiday."

I bit my lip before I spat out the words I really wanted to yell. I knew what he was saying. *You're fat and unfit. You're slow when you hike, and you couldn't climb a mountain if your life depended on it. You'll just be in the way.*

It was true. I knew that. I was overweight and unfit. I couldn't keep up with them. But the fact that they hadn't even asked me to come along was like a dagger slicing along my skin. More proof that if I didn't conform to their ideals then I didn't fit in the family. Anger surged. This was so fucking typical.

"It's fine, Dad." I spat back. "You guys enjoy your *family* holiday. I'll still be here when you get back." Because where the hell else would I be, right? Rage and hurt swirled through me, a deadly mix, and I forced myself to walk away before I said something that would permanently damage someone.

Because if I kept going, and destroyed my crumbling link with my family, I would be the only one who cared.

3

Wednesdays were my favourite day of the week. I taught three classes in the mornings, and even though there were rarely more than five bodies in the room, people still counted on me to show up. And the extra exercise always improved my mood. But it was Wednesday afternoons I loved the most. That was when I got to see my kids.

I loved those kids more than life itself. Right now, however, if they didn't move their asses down these stairs and into my ute, we'd all be late and my favourite day would lose a little of its shine. I wasn't in the mood for bad days. There had been too many of those lately. I needed a win. I still hadn't quite worked out what the hell had gone on with the woman from the gynaecology practice last week, but she'd cost me a client, wasted my time, and I was still kinda pissed off about it. I needed every new member I could get. With the bank getting impatient over late payments, I couldn't afford to be wasting time with women who played games.

So why couldn't I stop thinking about her? I'd tried telling myself it was just her baffling behaviour that had my gaze straying to the doors of the gynaecology practice whenever I had a spare moment. But there was something more than that. I was intrigued.

I pulled myself back into the present, before my daydreams made us late. "Ayva! Camden! Move it or lose it!"

Ayva thundered down the stairs, a tiny tornado of fair hair and sports bags, with a ukulele stuffed under one arm. She stopped in front of me, and I raised an eyebrow at her. "What's with the ukulele?

"I wrote a song for you. I'm going to play it on the way to Taekwondo lessons."

Well that sounded...delightful. I smiled at the pure enthusiasm radiating from her. My eardrums would likely bleed, because while Ayva was a kickass little ninja, singing was not her forte. But I didn't care one bit. Losing my hearing was worth seeing that look on her face. "Sounds great. I can't wait to hear it."

She scampered down the concrete steps and off toward the car.

"Where's your brother?" I called after her.

She shrugged and I tossed her the keys to my car. "Get in, I'll find him."

I jogged up the stairs, bypassing rooms I'd once lived in, until I reached Camden's. I paused in the doorway. He'd had the same bedroom ever since his mother and I had brought him home from hospital eleven years ago. His room had undergone a few changes over the years, changing from nursery, to toddler, to little boy. Most recently, it had been updated to reflect his official tween status. I'd painted these walls the deep navy blue he'd been so desperate for just a few weeks before I'd moved out.

"Hey, kid," I said, ruffling his hair. He batted my hand away and went back to tying his shoes. "You nearly ready? Your sister is already in the car and we need to get to the gym. I've got a few things to set up." I eyed the school uniform he was still wearing.

"Don't forget to pack your stuff for class tonight, hey? You can get changed when we get there."

"I know," he mumbled. But he didn't make any move to hurry and finish tying his laces. I sighed. This complete lack of conversation had been pretty standard, ever since his mother and I had split six months earlier. Ayva had taken our soon-to-be-final divorce in stride with a shrug of her shoulders. But Camden never spoke about it at all. Or maybe, he just didn't speak to me.

"Everything okay at school?"

"Fine."

"Your friends all good?"

"Yeah."

Right. Well. I'd tried.

Camden grabbed his backpack from the floor and pushed past me. I spotted his white Taekwondo uniform poking out from under the bed, and I grabbed it before following him down the stairs. At the bottom, I tossed the uniform to him. "You forgot this."

He caught it, before shoving it into his backpack. "Thanks."

"See you later, Jane!" I yelled to my ex who was somewhere in the back of the house, probably avoiding me, and pulled the door shut.

I knew Jane and I had a pretty standard custody arrangement. Most men probably got even less time with their kids than I did. They probably didn't get to pick their kids up every Wednesday afternoon for dinner and their Taekwondo lesson. But for someone who, until six months ago, had been around for every minute of their lives, the new routine was a kick to the teeth. I hated not seeing them every day. It was why I'd stuck things out with Jane for so damn long. Years longer than we should have.

She'd been seeing someone else for the last eighteen months of our relationship.

I couldn't even bring myself to care. We were so over by that point, it had seemed a natural progression. I'd fought the divorce, not because I still loved my wife, but because I loved my children, and the thought of only seeing them every second weekend was unthinkable.

I'd slowly been adjusting to living alone, but I lived for my weekends, and Wednesdays. I had nothing else but work to fill my time, and work was in a pretty depressing state right now, with dwindling numbers and, therefore, a dwindling paycheck.

I made the short drive to the gym, with Ayva's singing and questionable ukulele playing as the soundtrack, before pulling the ute into my regular parking spot.

"Who's that, Dad?" Ayva chirped.

Surprise flickered through me. I didn't know how to even begin to explain that one, as I took in the redheaded woman who stood with her arms crossed defiantly underneath her breasts. I didn't know whether to laugh or be pissed that she'd shown her face again. But I was definitely interested in finding out why she had.

"You guys go inside. I know Anthony has chocolate stashed in the work fridge. Just don't get it on your uniforms."

The two of them ran into the gym without another thought to the woman staring me down through the windshield.

Shaking my head, I got out of the car, pocketing my keys as I went, and stopped in front of her. I didn't have much choice. She'd moved in front of the door. Her long, auburn hair fell down her back in soft waves, but the look on her face was anything but soft. Determination shone in her eyes, and I would have bet money that she had her molars ground together.

"Cleo Clour," I said when she didn't move.

"Cleo Tanner, actually," she said with a sass that almost made me smile. Almost.

"Fine then, Cleo Tanner. Come to waste some more of my time?"

She at least had the decency to blush. Her cheeks pinkened and my gaze drew to her mouth as she bit her lip. A full, glossy bottom lip I hadn't noticed last week. Round, blue eyes framed by dark, thick lashes stared up at me, and her skin was pale and creamy. For a brief, surprising moment, I wondered about all the skin hidden beneath that plain, navy blue work uniform. The thought made my balls ache. She was pretty. No doubt about that.

But it was more than just the fact that she was pretty. Something was different about her today. Today she had a fire in her eyes that burned as bright as her hair. And that alone interested me. I knew determination when I saw it. It was what fed my fighters. It was what fed me. Hers lured me in like a siren.

I leant forward, shamelessly invading her space, and watched as her eyes widened.

Huh. I had an effect on her.

Something smug and satisfied sparked to life in my chest.

With my lips mere inches from hers, she seemed frozen, just watching me as I moved in. The closer I got, the more I wondered how far she'd let me get. If I eliminated the gap between us entirely, would she stop me?

At the last moment, she put her hand up, her palm landing in the centre of my chest. "What are you doing?" she yelped.

I forced a questioning expression onto my face and motioned to the handle behind her. "Opening the door?"

"Oh," she said.

I could have sworn I detected a hint of disappointment, and I tucked that titbit away for future use. I waited for her to move aside so I could open the door, but she didn't. Her internal battle to make some sort of decision was written all over her face, but I'd had my moment of flirty fun. "Cleo. Door. Remember?"

"Right." She went to move aside, then changed her mind. "No, wait. Just let me tell you why I'm here."

I stepped back and folded my arms across my chest, in much the same way she had earlier. "Okay."

"I want to join the gym."

I raised an eyebrow. "You want to join the gym?"

"Yes."

"What happened since last week when you hated gyms? I'm pretty sure your exact words were, *you couldn't pay me to train in there.*"

She rolled her eyes. "Not even close to anything I said. In fact, that's probably the worst paraphrasing ever."

I shrugged. "Still. You were pretty clear."

"I need to lose some weight and get fit."

I knew I was being an unprofessional prick, but I couldn't stop my eyes from roaming down her body. She was all tits and ass. Beneath that uniform, I would have bet good money she had curves for days. My fingers itched to tug off her jacket and strip her from the hideous clothes—find out exactly how curvy she was. In my opinion, she looked perfect.

But she hadn't asked for my opinion.

I reluctantly lifted my gaze to her eyes and found her creamy skin flushed pink. "If you want to get fit, yeah, I can help with that."

A flash of uncertainty seemed to catch her off balance, but in the next second that determination was back. She nodded fiercely. "Sign me up."

"Okay, then. Gym only?"

She frowned. "No, I want to train."

I quirked an eyebrow. "Really?"

She nodded.

"Boxing, Taekwondo, or mixed?"

"Taekwondo," she replied without hesitation.

"Personals or group classes?"

"Do you do the personals?" Her big, blue eyes stared up at me.

The corner of my lip lifted. "Some."

She pulled a face. "No, then. Group is fine."

I smirked. If she wanted to play it like that, hey, I could chase. "I take the group classes too, you know? There's a class at seven tonight. You should come."

She started to shake her head, but then something changed her mind. "Fine. I will. I'll see you tonight."

I nodded and watched her walk across the parking lot, back to her work. She probably wouldn't come. We'd had plenty of those over the years, but I found myself hoping she would. There was something behind that fire in her eyes and I wanted to know what.

I opened the gym door with a lightness I hadn't felt in some time. Wednesdays just kept getting better and better.

4

———

I was an idiot. An impulsive, foolish idiot. I'd spent two days stewing on the fact that my entire family thought me too pathetic to even invite on their trip. I'd barely slept, tossing and turning and playing the scene over and over again in my head. My brothers and Dad had all looked so guilty, but one thing burned in my mind. Not one of them, even when caught out, had suggested I should come.

They didn't want me there, slowing them down and putting a dampener on their trip. My brothers preferred to hang out with our *father* rather than me.

So screw them. They didn't have to want me around. But their pitying gazes had pissed me off. They could take their pity and shove it where the sun didn't shine. They were right. I was unfit. I couldn't keep up with them.

But I would. I would change that.

So, running on too many shots of espresso and partially delirious from lack of sleep, I'd found myself in front of Beau's gym, demanding he sign me up for classes. Which had seemed all well and good at the time, but now, standing in the corner of the waiting room, in Lycra gym clothes that probably showed off every cellulite dimple on my ass, I was decidedly less convinced.

Tonight the gym was much busier than it'd been when I'd "dropped the mail" off last week. For the last twenty minutes, I'd huddled in this corner, watching members come in. I hadn't thought it possible to be more ripped than Beau was, but I'd been wrong. Some of these guys put him to shame. They swaggered in, with boxing gloves hanging out of their gym bags. There were a lot of handshakes and man-hugs as the foyer began to fill with fighters waiting for their classes. There were some women too, which made me feel slightly more at ease, but we were few and far between.

Behind the glass wall that separated the foyer area from the training mats, Beau led two kids through a complicated series of kicks. The little girl couldn't have been older than eight, but she was a brutal little ninja, with her yells echoing from the rafters of the gym. She was the very definition of tiny but fierce. I'd been a tiny little ninja like her once too. But a joy shone in her eyes, and her grin was ear to ear as she went through her patterns.

I doubted I'd ever looked that happy on a gym floor.

The expression I could relate to was that of the older boy. He went through the motions, but his eyes were lifeless, his expression blank. His moves were all muscle memory and no effort. Beau circled him, gesturing as he explained how the boy could improve. I couldn't hear his words, but the longer they talked, the more frustrated Beau seemed to get. After his talking to, the boy stormed out, and Beau stood stiffly. The little girl went to run after him, but Beau stopped her, guiding her back to the mats, and they continued their lesson.

I bit my lip. I remembered having spats like that with my coach. It wasn't uncommon when you trained a lot. The thing that wasn't typical about the whole situation was the hurt expression on Beau's face. Coaches were a tough breed in general, in my experience. They were all about the sport. About mastering the techniques and becoming the best. There was very little care for the tantrums of athletes. The fact that Beau looked so hurt by the boy storming off only made me like him more.

Which was bad. Because the way he'd looked at me earlier had left me distracted for the rest of the day. I'd replayed the way he'd leaned in close. The way his eyes had travelled my body. Had I imagined it? Because it had felt distinctly like he'd been checking me out. But maybe he checked out all potential clients like that? Maybe all he saw was a body that needed training. That was his business, after all.

The minute hand on the clock mounted in the waiting area ticked over to seven, and the dozen people around me shuffled to the door of the workout room. I followed suit, my heart rate increasing with each step. The others spread out around the room, dropping their towels and water bottles close to the wall and toeing their shoes off. I copied their actions, finding a back corner of the room for myself, neatly pressing my socks into my shoes. My breath caught as I took my first step onto the padded mats. My weight sunk into them, the texture beneath my feet so familiar, though it had been many years since I'd stood on mats identical to these.

I surveyed the room, taking in the individual warm-ups of each fighter. Some bounced on their toes, moving from side to side. Some sat to stretch. I didn't know what to do. Did I follow? I hadn't done any sort of exercise class since I was fifteen. I'd probably pop a hamstring just from watching them if I wasn't careful.

The gazes of the other people in the room heated my skin. They tried to hide it, but I clearly stuck out. These people were lean, ripped, and moving like their warm-ups were an Olympic event. While I stood in the back—short, stumpy, and wishing I was anywhere but here. This had been a mistake. This class—this whole gym probably—was too advanced for me. I needed some nice little beginner class. Maybe water aerobics or something. What on earth had I been thinking, signing up at a martial arts gym?

Beau whistled through his teeth, getting the attention of each person in the room, then made a circling motion with his hand. Everyone took off, jogging around the edges of the mats. Oh God. Running. Why?

Trying to find my backbone, I forced myself to jog after them. But in less than one lap around the large room, three people had overtaken me and I was panting as loud as a dog on a hot day. My belly jiggled, my thighs rubbed together, and I just knew everyone was staring at me. Everyone could see it. This was mortifying. I didn't think it possible, but this was actually more embarrassing than the first day I'd come here and renamed myself Cleo Clour. Shit.

I finished a second lap of the room, and as I passed my towel and joggers in the back corner, I scooped them up and ran for the door. Slipping out, I made a beeline for the exit to the building. My cheeks flamed. And all these glass walls meant every person in there knew I was chickening out as well. I didn't know what was worse. Staying or leaving.

"Cleo."

I closed my eyes as fingers grasped my wrist, and Beau's deep voice wrapped around me like a blanket.

"Cleo," he said again. "Stop. Where are you going?"

I turned slowly. "Home?" I asked hopefully.

"But why?"

"Because all of that—" I motioned to the room that was now full of crazy people doing burpees with smiles on their faces "—is a bit much for me."

Beau looked over his shoulder at his class. "Just go at your own pace. No one is watching you."

Easy for him to say. He fit right in here. He wasn't the fat, self-conscious chick who couldn't even make it through a warm-up without huffing and puffing.

I gave him a pleading look. "I can't. Just let me go."

He squinted at me, then shook his head. "No."

"No?"

"You heard me. No. Come on." He tugged me back toward the class, and I had no choice but to follow him. That didn't stop me from protesting loudly while I slapped at his hand, not that he seemed to notice.

He stuck his head in the door. "Anthony," he said to a young guy in the front row. The man's tanned skin was covered in black and grey tattoos, and he had his long, dark hair scraped back into a ponytail. He raised an eyebrow in Beau's direction.

"Take the class today, yeah? I need to do something."

Anthony gave him a strange look, but then shrugged and nodded, like taking the class while Beau chased after runaway students was a normal occurrence. He moved to the front of the room, into the spot Beau had been occupying, but I didn't see what happened next as I was tugged further into the building. I'd stopped complaining once I realised he wasn't going to force me back into class, but when he pulled me through a door marked Staff Only, I wondered what the hell was going on. Maybe this is where he took people to cancel their memberships?

But on the other side, instead of an office, I found myself in a smaller workout room. This one had no windows. It was completely closed in by solid walls, lit only by artificial light.

"Is this where you take the bad students to punish them?" I only half joked. It did have a bit of a dungeon-type feel.

Beau crossed his arms over his large chest and eyed me carefully. "Is that what you need? Punishing?"

My face heated. Because suddenly my brain was full of the dirtiest thoughts imaginable. I'd seen *Fifty Shades of Grey*. I could get on board with that sort of punishing.

"I, um..." Crap! What did he want me to say?

"I'm joking, Cleo."

"Oh." I wasn't sure if I was relieved or disappointed.

"You're uncomfortable in front of a roomful of people. I get it. So train here, with me. Personals."

"What about your class?"

Beau shrugged. "Anthony works for me. We swap our shifts around as needed to fit in with our personal clients. He'll cover."

"Oh."

"So?"

My brain was scrambling at being in such close quarters with him. This was *such* a bad idea. I'd never be able to concentrate when I was locked in a room with *him* for an hour at a time. And I probably couldn't afford the additional cost for private lessons. But I didn't want to go back to the main class either. The only other option was leaving. Did I really want to keep going on the way I had been? Too unfit to keep up with my family? The burning embarrassment I'd felt as my brothers made plans without me, spurred me on.

I stuck my hand out for him to shake and tried not to react as his skin touched mine. "Personals. Deal."

5

I was in a world of trouble. Personals with Beau turned out to be, well, personal. He took me through a quick warm-up, which thankfully didn't include burpees. Then got me moving with some simple punch/kick combos. Combos I'd done hundreds, if not thousands, of times when I'd been younger. At first, my muscles resisted, the movements stiff and jerky. My brain knew what to do, but my body—too used to sitting at a reception desk all day—was rebelling. I kicked the foam paddles Beau held for me, frustration with myself rising with each kick I couldn't get quite right.

Beau dropped his arms. "Stop. Why are you pissed off right now?"

My chest heaved as I tried to catch my breath. "I just want to do it better."

A tiny smile tugged up the corner of Beau's lips. "Well, that's a turn around from an hour ago when you wanted to leave."

I shrugged. "A girl can change her mind, can't she?"

His smile turned into a wide grin. "Nothing hotter than a determined woman."

I froze. Was he calling me hot?

But he didn't seem to think anything of the comment, so I brushed it off.

"You're doing amazingly well for a beginner. Quit being so hard on yourself. You don't have to be perfect tonight."

I opened my mouth to tell him that I did need to be perfect, though. You didn't win if you weren't. That old pressure my father had shoved down my throat reared its ugly head. I should tell Beau who I was. Tell him why, even though I was unfit, I was maybe a bit better than the average beginner. But then he'd have expectations of me. There'd be that pressure to be the same fighter I'd been when I was fifteen. I wasn't her anymore. I didn't *want* to be. That girl had been miserable. Those old thoughts and feelings weren't welcome here in this safe space Beau had carved out for me. Beau didn't need to know who I had once been. Just like it wasn't my father's business if I was training again. If he knew, he'd insist I train with him, and that was the absolute last thing I wanted. No. I didn't owe either of them any sort of explanation. This was something I could do for me, and me alone.

Beau led me through a cool down, then motioned toward a bench on the side of the room where we'd left our water bottles. I sat down on the opposite end of the bench to him, all too aware that I'd been working out for an hour and probably smelled ripe. As it was, sweat dripped down my back, and I knew my face had to be red and blotchy. Not exactly a good look.

But Beau slid along the seat, stopping mere inches from me. My skin prickled with awareness. He'd barely broken a sweat, so he still smelled fresh and clean. I dared a peek at him from the corner of my eye. I hadn't forgotten how attractive he was. But trying to master the moves Beau had demonstrated had become my top priority, everything else being pushed into the background.

But now that we'd stopped, it was all I could think of.

"Give me your hand."

"Geez, Beau. Buy a girl a drink before you ask for her hand," I joked. Then abruptly shut my mouth. What if he was married? I hadn't seen a wedding ring, but he wore no other jewellery either, so maybe he just took it off to train.

Making jokes about giving him my hand in marriage would be incredibly inappropriate and downright disrespectful if he had a wife. I tensed. He probably did have someone. Decent, good-looking guys in their mid-thirties weren't single long. And he seemed to be all those things. No one had forced him to run after and convince me to go back to class. He didn't have to see that the group class wasn't right for me and offer up personals. Sure, maybe he had motivation in the fact that I'd be paying him. But there was something more than that. Something in the way he'd remembered my name. Something in the way his fingers had wrapped around my wrist, and how he hadn't taken no for an answer. Something about him screamed that he cared. Probably not just about me. He cared about his students—that was obvious. The hurt on his face when that boy had left his class and the way he'd taken time to speak to the girl afterwards all told me he was a good coach. A good man.

"I meant give me your hands and I'll unstrap your gloves for you."

Oh.

I could have done it myself. But he was offering.

I held the hand closest to him out, letting him rip off the Velcro straps and tug the glove off my hand. He did the same with the other, and I watched curiously as he freed them. I flexed my fingers instinctively but didn't pull away. And he made no move to drop them. He ran his fingertips over my palms before turning my hands over. His thumb brushed over my knuckles, and my breath hitched at the feather-light touch.

"Your knuckles are scratched up from the gloves," he said quietly.

Were they? I'd been so lost in the feel of his hands on mine that I hadn't even noticed. Red marks marred the skin on the back of my fingers. Barely scratches really. But he held my hands like they were delicate. I glanced up and caught him studying me.

Our gazes collided, my heart thumping in my chest. He was so close I could see the specks of hazel in his green eyes.

He didn't look down but brushed over my ring finger. "Not married?"

I shook my head quickly. "No."

"Seeing anyone?"

I swallowed hard before I spoke again. "No."

My mind whirled. "Are you?" I choked out, hating that I would be blushing red. Damn pale skin. Maybe he wouldn't notice, what with being flushed from exercise. But my face was so hot you could cook an egg on it.

"I—"

"Dad! There you are!"

Beau jumped away from me as if he'd been stung, dropping my hands. I spun around to see the little girl from the class before mine. She was still kitted out in her training gear, but now she stood with her hands on her hips, glaring up at her father. "Mum's here."

Beau glanced at me and then back at his daughter. "Tell her I'll be there in a minute. I'm just finishing up a personal lesson."

"Okay!" The little girl flounced away, and I looked down at the floor in a mix of embarrassment and astonishment. Why was he asking me if I was single when he clearly was very *not* single?

"Okay, well, I'm going to get out of here and leave you to your family. Thanks for the lesson, Beau." I got up stiffly and moved toward the exit, unreasonably disappointed. I was an idiot for thinking he'd been flirting with me. To think that the way he'd looked me up and down had meant anything.

"See you next week? Same time?" he called after me.

I nodded, not really trusting myself to speak when I wasn't sure what would come out. Anger? Disappointment? I'd be fine by next week's personal.

I passed Beau's daughter in the foyer, sitting with the older boy who I now assumed to be Beau's son. They were drawing in sketchbooks, pencils spread out around them. I paused, catching sight of the incredibly detailed dragon the boy had drawn. The beast's majestic wings spread wide across the page, the use of shading to show light seemingly advanced for a child his age. Not that I knew anything about kids.

"That's amazing," I murmured to him, unable to stop myself.

He shrugged, then closed the book.

Well, if that wasn't a clear sign I'd overstepped, I didn't know what was. The girl didn't look up, but the boy watched me leave. I gave him a small smile and pushed through the door into the night air.

On the other side, a woman held her phone to her ear, while she yelled at whomever was on the other end. She had to be Beau's wife. She was exactly the type I would have pigeon-holed him with. Tall, blond, and completely put together in expensive-looking clothes. She'd had two kids and still had a tiny waist and perky boobs. I hadn't had any, but my boobs sat heavy, and no amount of push-up bras was going to make them sit as nicely as this woman's little B cup.

She didn't pay any attention to me, and I hurried across the dark parking lot to where I'd left my car. This day had been confusing, and it was time to go home. Go home, get into bed, and pray I didn't dream of Beau.

I pulled my keys from my bag, fumbling with them, trying to sort through the various shapes and sizes for the key I needed.

The key chain slipped through my fingers. Despite my best efforts to catch it on its way down, it hit the ground with a clang.

Wait. That clanging sound wasn't right. That wasn't the sound of keys hitting the concrete.

I knelt, my fingers finding the metal grate of a stormwater drain. With a sinking feeling, I switched on my phone's torch.

Sure enough, my car keys sat neatly at the bottom of the drain. The *locked with a padlock* drain.

Great. Just fucking great.

6

———

After I sent the kids off with their mother, I walked around the gym, double-checking everyone had left, and that Anthony had turned all the lights out. It took less than five minutes to count up the measly amount of cash, and I sighed as the end-of-day report printed. The figures were pretty sad. I shoved the report into its folder and punched in the alarm code to activate it. Not that anyone would get much if they did bother to break in.

I climbed into my ute and manoeuvred it around the unlit parking lot, the headlights bouncing off empty buildings. I rounded the shadowy corner by the gynaecology practice and squinted as the headlight illuminated a Lycra-clad figure sitting on the hood of her car.

Interesting.

I let the car slow to a stop and wound down the window. "Do you make it a habit to hang out in this parking lot, waiting for me to show up?"

Cleo scowled, then pushed herself off the hood of her car and walked stiffly over to me. "I dropped my car keys down the drain."

"Shit. Did you call someone?"

She shrugged. "I didn't want to call roadside assist. I'm not a member so it'll cost a fortune. And...well, I called my boss and his girlfriend, but they didn't answer, and I didn't really have anyone else. So I ordered an Uber."

I frowned but didn't comment on the fact that she'd had no family or close friends to call on in an emergency. Maybe they lived out of town.

"Get in."

"Hey?"

"Cleo, I'm not leaving you sitting on your car in a pitch-black parking lot at 9pm. You have a spare house key somewhere?"

"In a flowerpot."

I didn't even comment on how unsafe that was. "Get in," I said again. "I'll drive you home."

She hesitated. "I'll get a bad Uber rating."

I stared at her.

"Okay, fine. Bossy much?"

I almost pointed out that I'd not been bossy at all, but she had grabbed her stuff and moved to the passenger side, so I'd already won the argument. She passed through the beam of headlights, and I watched in fascination as the light lit up her hair.

I'd wanted to run my fingers through that red hair all night. She wasn't the first newbie to walk out of one of my classes. Normally, I just let them go. They either came back and tried a different class, or they didn't. But with the downhill slide the gym's membership numbers had taken, I needed to make sure each and every member was satisfied.

At least, that's what I'd told myself. Keeping the customer was why I'd pulled her into the private training room, away from the stares of the other members. I was just being a good trainer. A good business owner.

Ha. Truth was, I'd watched her run out of the room and gone after her without even thinking about it. I'd never once asked Anthony to take over a class, then completely rearranged the schedule so I could do a personal session, even though I'd told her I had. That was ridiculous, and I'd known it from the strange look Anthony had given me. I'd have to talk to him about that tomorrow.

And now I was insisting on her getting in my car. I could have just waited with her, until her Uber showed up.

The passenger door opened, and Cleo hoisted herself in. Awareness prickled over me. How long had it been since I'd had a woman in this car?

"My house is on South Street," she said, startling me back into motion.

Right. *Drive the woman home, Beau. That's what you are supposed to be doing.*

I put the car in gear and pulled out onto the streetlight-lit road. We were quiet for a while, but the silence eventually got to me. I kept opening my mouth to ask her something, then realised it was a stupid question and closed it. I must have looked ridiculous, opening and closing my mouth like a fish gulping for air. I leant forward to switch the radio on, right as she asked, "Are you married?"

I pulled my hand away from the stereo controls. "Yes," I said truthfully. Then glanced over at her. Her mouth had pulled into a tight line, and I found myself wanting to reach out and smooth my thumb across her lips.

"That was your wife in the gym tonight? And your kids?"

I nodded and she turned to look out the window. I couldn't help the smile that lifted my mouth. I liked that she was pouting over me being married.

"I'm separated, though. We split six months ago, but we were over long before that. She's already moved on. We're just waiting on the divorce to be finalised."

Her gaze rested on me as I turned into her street.

"Oh. Sorry to hear that."

I stifled a laugh. She didn't sound all that sorry. She sounded decidedly more pleased than when I'd told her I was married.

She pointed to her place, a cute red brick that looked old but well loved, and I pulled over to the side of the suburban road. She gathered up her things, then paused with her hand on the door.

"I feel like this is the part where I'm supposed to invite you in."

I raised an eyebrow. "I think that's the closing line to a date, not a rescue ride home."

She scrunched her face up.

Shit. She was really kind of adorable.

"Yeah. You're right. Which makes this super awkward, so I'm going to leave now and lie awake all night, obsessing over how embarrassing this was."

I chewed my bottom lip. I could let her off the hook and tell her she had no reason to be embarrassed at all. Because just the mention of going upstairs with her had made me uncomfortably tight in the pants area. But she was too cute to let off the hook so easily, and a large part of me wanted her thinking about me all night. So instead I winked at her.

She turned away and shuffled out of the car.

I watched as she walked up the stairs to her front door. At the top, she looked back over her shoulder.

"Night, Cleo," I called, forcing myself to remain in my seat and start the engine again.

"Night, Beau."

$\mathcal{H}$ell was the morning after doing strenuous exercise for the first time in fifteen years. I couldn't move. Every muscle in my body hurt. Muscles I didn't even know I had, burned every time I tried to lift a limb. I'd run a bath for myself, but when I'd attempted to lift my legs high enough to climb in, they screamed in agony. I just couldn't do it. I'd had to settle for a hot shower, which had briefly helped, but by the time I'd pulled on my uniform and limped my way downstairs to wait for my Uber, any benefits from the warm water had worn off.

This was the thanks I got for exercising. My body officially hated me.

I shuffled out to the curb while scrolling through Facebook on my phone. Paragraphs deep into a rant by some woman I'd gone to high school with, I walked into a wall.

Strong hands caught me before I landed on my ass, and I looked up to realise I'd walked into a wall of Beau. My free hand flattened on his chest as I steadied myself, but I left it there longer than actually needed.

"Did you add stalker to your resume overnight?" I joked,

trying to force my hand to obey my commands to stop feeling the man up.

His palm slid along my arm, and his fingers wrapped around the handle of my bag, which had slipped from my shoulder. He moved it back to its rightful spot, brushing the side of my neck in the process. The sensation made me want to close my eyes and tilt my head to give him better access. If his fingers felt that good, what would his lips feel like?

As if he'd read my thoughts, he leaned in and said quietly, "It's only stalking if you don't like it, Cleo. And I think you do."

Woah. I'd thought there was some sort of vibe between us before. But this was straight out flirting. What did I do with that? Did I flirt back? I almost rolled my eyes even as the question passed through my head. *You haven't had a date in a year, Cleo. And look at the man. Of course you flirt back!*

I tossed my hair off my shoulders and opened my mouth to respond and...nothing. I had absolutely nothing witty, or charming, or flirty to say. Because I was bloody hopeless with men. Especially men who looked like Beau.

So instead, I asked the first thing that came to mind. "No, seriously. How come you're here?"

Smooth. Super smooth.

He straightened up, and the tension between us evaporated as quickly as it had appeared.

"We work in the same complex, and you said you didn't have anyone to call last night. I thought you might want a lift. I brought some tools as well, so we can try to rescue your keys."

I looked down at my feet to hide the massive smile that spread across my face. Good-looking and thoughtful. Aye. I didn't stand a chance.

I shuffled along beside him until we reached his ute. I looked up at the big truck and winced at the thought of trying to hoist my aching body into the cab.

"Why are you looking at my car like it's death on wheels? You drove with me last night and I stuck to the speed limit. You're safe with me."

Oh, I wasn't safe with him at all. But that's not what he meant.

"It's not that. I can barely walk this morning after the torture you inflicted on me last night."

"Ah, DOMS." He glanced down at me. "Delayed onset—"

"Muscle soreness. Yeah, I know what it is. Doesn't make it hurt any less though. And just the thought of climbing into this car makes me want to weep."

Beau moved in behind me, his fresh, clean, just-showered scent washing over me as he crowded my space. His fingers gripped my hips and he lifted me up into the cab.

I was sitting on the seat before I even really knew what had happened.

Beau shut my door, then jogged around to his side. A strange mix of emotions cascaded over me. Mortification over him lifting me. Now he knew exactly how heavy I was and how padded my hips were. I could have struggled into the car by myself. But at the same time, the memory of his hands on me, his chest pressed against my back...arousal bloomed low in my belly. I was so lost in the heat pulsing through me that I didn't notice anything outside of Beau and the way his presence made me feel. Until he groaned.

He slowed the car and I followed his line of vision as we passed the double-storey TAS Sports and Fitness building.

"Unfuckingbelievable."

Oh no. I ducked a little in my seat, praying he wasn't going to stop. But of course, he did.

"What are you doing?" I squeaked out. I dropped my sunglasses onto my face even though it was still too early to really need them. Who knew when one of my brothers would walk out of the gym and see me sitting in a car decorated with their competitor's logo. Trying to explain that one would make for the world's most awkward Sunday night dinner.

"Just checking out the competition. Look at that pretentious fucking display screen they've installed."

"Oh?" I feigned interest.

"I bet it cost fifty thousand."

Seventy-five actually, I corrected in my head. I knew exactly how much the "pretentious fucking display screen" had cost because my father had spoken of nothing else all last month when it was being installed.

"This place will be the death of my business," Beau said through gritted teeth. "The guy who runs it is a shark. I'm in the same fight division as his sons and they fight dirty. They're all about the win. There's no heart."

If only he knew.

"Every tournament I go to, he makes some crack about buying me out."

I cringed, praying Beau wouldn't connect the dots. Prayed he'd forgotten my surname. I knew I should say something. Tell Beau that I was the daughter and sister of those people he disliked so much. And hell, I should probably be upset that he was bagging my family out. But nothing he'd said was untrue. My father's gym *was* pretentious. And he did train his fighters— my brothers and the men and women who worked out there— to be winners at any cost.

I'd been like that once too.

So yeah, I should tell him who I was. But then this little flirtation between us would end. Beau would want to know why I was training with him instead of my father and that was a whole kettle of fish I wasn't ready to deal with. In that little room in Beau's gym, I'd been able to hide away and train like no one was watching. Like no one cared if I won or lost. Or if I even competed at all. And for the first time in as long as I could remember, I'd actually enjoyed exercising. My father had killed the love of the sport for me, but last night Beau had brought a little of it back into my life. I wasn't ready for that to stop yet.

"Beau? I'm going to be late for work if we sit here gawking at a building much longer." Lies. I had plenty of time. But I needed to change the topic. And that wasn't going to happen while we were sitting in front of my father's gym. I'd already told so many lies since I'd met Beau that in the scheme of untruths, this one was pretty small. I had to swallow down a lump of guilt anyway, though.

"Oh right, of course. Sorry." He pulled back into the traffic and finished the drive to work.

"Can you get down okay?" he asked when he stopped in front of the gynaecology doors. The engine idled quietly in the background.

There was genuine concern in his voice, but that was hard to deal with after lying to him. So I resorted to sarcasm. My trusty friend for when times were awkward. "Yes. Thank you. No need to be a hero this time."

He winked and my thighs clenched. I wished he'd stop doing that. It was entirely too sexy. I waved in his direction and shuffled my aching legs toward the clinic.

"Cleo?" Beau called.

I turned around to where he still sat in his ute. "Yeah?"

"What are you doing on your lunch break?"

I shrugged. "Eating?"

"Come by the gym. Get a massage. I'll book you an appointment. On the house."

"Um, okay?"

He chuckled. "It'll help with the stiffness."

Not really understanding why he was laughing, I nodded. A massage sounded amazing. "I'll be there."

He gave me a salute and drove his car across the lot to his designated parking spot. I let myself into the clinic, dropping my bag beneath my desk. It was only once I was sitting down that I realised I'd ditched yet another Uber. I groaned. I could probably faithfully assume my rating was in the toilet.

8

———

My lunch break couldn't come soon enough. My desk chair and I had become fast friends during the course of the morning. I'd tried standing up with my stiff muscles, but after nearly falling on my face, I'd decided I needed a wheelchair. Since a real wheelchair was a little dramatic for a case of DOMS, I'd made do with my desk chair. But even that didn't help escape all the pains. Lifting a stapler made me yelp.

Exercise was evil. If I hadn't enjoyed myself so much last night, I'd vow never to do it again. But I also knew this initial pain wouldn't last and the soreness after each session would lessen.

But still, I spent most of the morning daydreaming about my lunchtime massage.

When twelve o'clock rolled around, I quickly freshened my makeup, then limped across the complex to Beau's gym. Little butterflies rioted around my belly at the knowledge I'd see him again.

When I pushed through the gym doors, he looked up from behind the desk, and I nearly fainted as the sexiest grin I'd ever seen spread across his face. God. Did he smile at everyone like that? My stupid heart wanted to think he saved smiles that blinding just for me, but that was ridiculous. I'd had one tiny scrap of attention from the man and I was already fantasising about marrying him.

My head conjured up a heart-stopping image of me gliding down an aisle, wearing a beautiful lace gown with a train as long as the eye could see. Beau stood at the altar, smiling at me like I was the only woman on earth. Birds sang, the sun shined, and the crowd around us oohed and aahed over how perfect we were together.

And then a black storm cloud rolled in, opening on me before I could reach his outstretched hand. My father and brothers blocked the aisle, their low voices accusing me of sleeping with the enemy. *Liar*, they all chanted. *Liar*. Over and over again until eventually, Beau joined in.

I blinked hard, the image dissolving. Beau watched me curiously. My cheeks went hot.

"Hey!" I said brightly. Too brightly.

"You okay? You looked lost there for a moment."

I shook my head. "Nope, I'm fine. Just eager to get this massage."

He nodded and pointed down the hallway. "Massage room is next to the training room we were in last night. You remember how to get there?"

"Sure."

He picked up a pen and scratched something out on a pad of paper as he talked. "Go on down, I'll be with you in five minutes, just let me jot this order down."

I took three steps in the direction he'd pointed before his words really registered. I spun back around.

"*You'll* be with me in five minutes? You're the masseuse?"

He glanced up, his eyebrows drawn together adorably. "Yeah? Is that okay?"

I moved my head up and down rapidly but, on the inside, I was screaming, *no, no no!* I smiled weakly and followed the hallway down past the room we'd trained in last night. Beau was the masseuse? Oh my God. The thought had not even crossed my mind. Maybe I'd misunderstood him? Because I could not get a massage from that man. Shit!

An open door with a massage table in the middle told me I'd found the right room. I wandered in, walking slowly around the edges. Dim light revealed framed photos of tranquil-looking rainforests hanging from the walls. It was a pretty half-assed attempt at decorating. Beau's qualification certificates hung in matching frames, and I sighed. Definitely no misunderstanding. My aching muscles wanted to cry at the thought of turning around and leaving, but I couldn't do this. Not with Beau.

"Hey," he said quietly, leaning on the doorjamb. He pointed at a towel on the bed. "Strip off and lie down with the towel covering you. I'll be back in a minute to get started."

Before I could complain, he closed the door. For a long moment I just stared at the towel on the table and wondered what the hell I was going to do now? I could run. Again. But Beau had already proved he was happy to chase me down. Or I could just get undressed, get under the towel, and pretend it wasn't Beau touching me.

Resigned, I undid the buttons on my work blouse, moving rapidly now that I'd decided I was going through with it. Because the thought of Beau walking back in that door and catching me standing here half naked was a lot more mortifying than being naked under the towel. I haphazardly folded my blouse and skirt, leaving them on a chair before toeing off my shoes. Taking a deep breath, I undid my bra and pulled the cups away, my breasts feeling full and heavy. I looked up at the roof and closed my eyes. My nipples had hardened at the thought of being naked in here, with only a thin piece of wooden door separating us. I hooked my fingers in my underwear, then paused. Was I supposed to take those off too? I'd never had a massage before. And Beau hadn't specified.

Wracking my brain, I tried desperately to conjure up what the protocol was from movies or books I'd read, but I really had no idea. Oh, fuck it. He was going to be back here any second. *Just make a decision, Cleo!* I shucked my underwear, shoving it under my skirt on the chair right as Beau knocked on the door. With a yelp of panic I dove for the bed, yanking the towel up over me, and slammed my face down in the hole.

"You ready?" Beau called as my heart slammed against my chest.

"Yes," I called. More lies. I was anything but ready.

His sneakers squeaked slightly on the floorboards, and he moved around the bed, past my clothes. I squeezed my eyes shut as I heard him preparing massage oil, and braced myself for the feel of his hands on my skin. This was not how I'd imagined it. In my dreams, this scenario would have been super sexy. I wouldn't have even bothered with a towel. I would have just laid myself bare for him and been aching for his touch. Bold and full of a confidence that I certainly didn't feel in this moment.

I didn't hate my body. But I didn't love it either. I had cellulite on my thighs and rolls on my tummy. I avoided sleeveless shirts because my arms jiggled. I was about to bare all of that to a man who made my heart skip a beat every time he was near. A man who was as solid as a wall. Who probably had 2% body fat. If we'd been in the darkness of his bedroom, I would have been nervous enough, but this was so much worse. This almost felt like an examination.

"Okay, I'm going to start at your neck and move my way down."

I tried to nod my head, but the table made that difficult. Beau didn't seem to notice. His warm fingers slicked with oil moved over my neck, rubbing little circles over the strained muscles on either side of my spine. I barely noticed, as I tried to calm my breathing, keeping it even and regular. I didn't want to give away how nervous I was by breathing like I'd just run a marathon. I stared hard at his feet, trying to concentrate on anything but the feel of his hands on my skin. He had big feet. Which meant he probably had a big…

Nope. Don't think about that. I squeezed my eyes tight again, but now all I could think of was Beau and his probably giant cock. Beau stroking it. *Me* stroking it. Oh my God.

Beau moved his nimble fingers down to my shoulders, and a groan escaped my mouth.

"You particularly sore there?" he asked quietly.

I murmured an affirmative sound because I wasn't about to tell him what I was really thinking.

Beau increased the pressure and I realised that he was actually really good at this. His massage verged on painful, but it was a good kind of pain. The kind I needed to get rid of the kinks in my shoulders after last night's workout. He shifted down my back, lowering the towel as he went, until only my backside was covered. His fingers travelled down my skin, pushing through each sore muscle in turn, relaxing me more with each stroke. I knew he'd be able to see at least a little bit of side boob, but the more he kneaded my flesh, the less I cared. My eyes fluttered closed, and the muscles in my face, which had been tense since he walked in, smoothed out. He worked on my back just long enough for me to begin to feel sleepy. God. His wife was a stupid woman. Why you'd break up with a man who looked like him and could give massages like this, was beyond my comprehension.

"I'm going to start on your legs."

I didn't bother answering. I was in some state of complete and utter bliss. Why had I never had a massage before?

Beau lifted one foot, then trailed his hands up and down my calf. Each time he reached my knee, his fingers inched just a little higher up my thigh, and with each movement, my awareness came back to me. The tips of his fingers were mere inches from my very core, and a fire began burning deep within. Daydreams of his fingers slipping beneath the towel, stroking high up my inner thigh and finding that place in between flashed behind my eyes. His thick fingers would slip through the wetness building there, and then he'd push up inside me, making me cry out when he found my most sensitive spots.

Beau coughed, and I came slamming back down to earth. I lifted my head and looked over my shoulder at him.

"Uh, you're all finished."

Oh.

He turned away to wash his hands, then moved to the door. "I'll let you get dressed."

As he slipped out, his eyes caught mine. For the briefest moment, his gaze was so raw and full of...something. Something primal that took my breath away. Lust? Need? But then he was gone, and I sat up, wrapping the towel around myself.

No. That was ridiculous. I'd seen his type. His ex was long and leggy and put together. I was short, chubby, and a bit of a hot mess. I was projecting my own feelings onto him. Maybe seeing things in him that I wanted to see. Things that might not really be there. And even if they were, what the hell was I supposed to do with that? I couldn't ask him if he wanted to devour me the way I wanted to devour him. Blood rushed to my face just thinking about saying that out loud.

I slipped from the table and quickly threw my clothes back on. Scuttling back to the reception foyer, I marvelled at the way I could now walk without limping. Beau knew his stuff, that was for sure.

Relief filled me when I noticed he was on a call. No chance

to make stilted small talk. So instead I waved awkwardly. He nodded and I made my exit.

Outside, I sucked in a deep lungful of fresh air as a shit-eating grin spread across my face. I knew I'd be reliving that massage in every dream I had from now until

eternity.

9

Cleo disappeared through the gym entrance, and I slowly put the phone down, feeling like a fool. What was I, fifteen? What kind of grown man picked up a phone and pretended to be on a call just to avoid speaking to a woman?

But I'd needed a minute to get myself under control. I'd massaged a lot of women and men over the years. It was part of my job and I'd always been a complete professional about it.

Until today.

Today, Cleo's creamy skin, the softness of her body, and the feel of her beneath my fingers had nearly undone me. I'd seen her plain black underwear, poking out from beneath her pile of work clothes, and from the minute I'd realised she was completely naked beneath that towel, I'd struggled to keep myself in check. I'd had to fight back the urge to flip her onto her back and massage her breasts. I'd wanted to run my hands down over her stomach and below the towel, so I could get at every inch of her. When I'd suggested she come for a massage, I hadn't even been thinking. I'd enjoyed her company, and she was hurting after I'd worked her hard last night. It seemed like the natural thing to do. It's what I would have offered any gym client.

I hadn't anticipated the way her scent would engulf the tiny room. Or the way she made tiny noises of pleasure that she seemed completely unaware of. I wasn't prepared for how downright, fucking sexy those noises were and how my cock would react to them in a completely unprofessional manner. I hadn't anticipated having to massage her longer than normal just to give myself time to get *that* situation under control.

Fuck. I hadn't had sex in months. Not since before Jane and I split. Women had tried. But the interest just hadn't been there on my part. They were all women from the gym. Some were pretty, sure. They were fit and toned, and we maybe had some stuff in common, what with martial arts and tournaments.

But they just reminded me of Jane. And Jane wasn't what I wanted. She hadn't been what I wanted for a long time now. I was too old to just have a superficial relationship. That's what Jane and I had had, really. And it was why we hadn't lasted the distance. I didn't want to spend all my time obsessing over food and training. I wasn't twenty anymore. I wanted something deeper. Sure, I still wanted to be attracted to the woman I ended up with, but I wanted someone that made me laugh. Someone kind. Someone who could be a friend as well as a lover.

I watched Cleo walk across the complex and wondered if I'd found all of those things in the woman who worked across the road.

*t 5pm, I left Anthony and one of our part-time staff members to run the gym and grabbed my toolbox from the back of the ute.

I made it over to Cleo's car right as she left the gynaecology practice. I'd googled its closing time, and hoped she was in charge of locking up. She stopped when she saw me, and I held up my tools. "Thought you might want a hand getting your keys out of the drain?"

Her smile was infectious. She sauntered over and I couldn't help but let my eyes run over her. I wanted to see her in something other than that hideous uniform. Hell, who was I kidding. I wanted to see her in lacy black lingerie. I wanted to see her naked. And not the covered-up, professional kind of naked I'd seen today. I wanted her stripped bare and on display. For me. And only for me.

Fuuuuccckk. I needed to stop thinking like that before I had to fake another phone call in order to get my erection under control.

She perched on the bonnet of her car, while I knelt on the ground and studied the drain. Cleo's keys, with a large golden C on the keyring, still sat in a neat pile at the bottom. The drain was screwed down, but it looked pretty simple to take apart.

"You didn't have to do this, you know? Don't you have anything better to do than dismantle drains for me?"

I shrugged. The late afternoon sun made her hair glow like a goddess, all backlit by the dying light. I forced my concentration to the drain, ignoring the urge to push her back across that bonnet, public setting be damned. If I let my body have its way, I'd be doing a whole lot more than massaging her.

If only.

"I don't have much of a life, outside the gym," I replied instead, while telling myself to think unsexy thoughts. Drain sludge. That's what I needed to be thinking about right now. The nasty drain sludge I was about to stick my hand in. Not getting it on with Cleo.

"So you aren't taking advantage of your newly found single status and partying it up like some frat boy?"

I laughed. "Hardly. No, I'm much more the 'stay home and eat pizza with the kids' type of guy."

"I saw your kids last night at the gym. They're adorable."

I squinted at her. "Thanks. Ayva's a little spitfire. She's a whirlwind to parent, but she's an open book so that makes life easier. Camden is harder. I think he's reached 'that age' where I'm not cool anymore, and he wants nothing to do with me."

I'd meant it as an offhand remark, but the words stung anyway. Camden had walked out of class, not for the first time, last night. I needed to talk to him about that, because as his coach I deserved more respect. But as his father, I was worried. As it was, I never saw him and Ayva anymore. Well, not never, but certainly nowhere near as often as I liked. And he was such a good little fighter. We had a tournament coming up that could bring the club some real publicity. We needed that. As a coach and business owner, I needed Camden to want to win. As his dad, I just wanted him to be there. If he stopped coming to class, that was yet another day I'd miss seeing him. He was already far too grown up. I didn't want to miss what was left of his childhood.

I grabbed my drill, switched it to reverse, and began removing the screws from the grate. It was noisy, but that didn't bother Cleo. She just raised her voice to talk over the racket it made.

"So. Staying home with the kids is your idea of a big night? How does your girlfriend feel about that?"

I stopped drilling. "What girlfriend?"

She shrugged. "I just assumed you had one. You know, looking like..." She trailed off and motioned up and down.

I removed the last screw. "What does that mean?"

She rolled her eyes. "Don't pretend like you don't know you're attractive."

"Why not? You do."

She stopped swinging her legs. "You think I'm attractive?"

I fished the keys out of the drain and wiped them off on my pants before I stood. "Yeah, Cleo. I do." My voice came out gruffer than I'd intended. I swallowed hard. Would now be the time to ask her out? I hadn't asked a woman out in over fifteen years. I had no idea how to read the situation.

At least she thought I was attractive. That was a start.

I inched closer, loving the way her head tilted to look up at me. It would be so easy to take one more step. To lean in and kiss a trail down her neck. To watch her head drop back as I found the sensitive spots beneath her ear, and to listen to her breaths increase as I whispered every dirty thought I'd been thinking since last night.

Instead I held her keys out.

She reached to take them from me, and I dropped them into her palm.

"Thank you. Not just for getting the keys. For this morning. And last night. I think I owe you a beer."

Her cheeks went pink.

I liked how that looked on her. "You asking me out, Cleo?"

She shook her head quickly, then looked down at her lap. "Oh, no. I just..."

I shrugged. "I'll ask you then. Want to go for a beer sometime? You do owe me one."

I grinned as she lifted her head, a small smile tilting the corners of her mouth.

"When?"

"Tonight, tomorrow, next week. Whenever."

She thought that over for a minute, then her grin widened, and she jumped off the car. "Sunday. I know the perfect place."

I opened my mouth to agree, then grimaced. "Sunday is—"

"Oh, that's okay," she shook her head. "If it's not a good day for you—"

"No, it's just..." I ran my hands through my hair and squinted at her. "Sunday is my birthday."

"So you have plans?"

"Actually, no. My kids are with their mother." I thought that over for a minute. Did I really want to sit at home by myself on my first birthday post separation and be bummed out that my kids weren't with me?

No. I really didn't. Because that was incredibly pathetic. "Sunday is good. I'll pick you up. Seven?"

She bit her lip as she got into her car. For a second, I thought she was going to change her mind. But then she nodded. She started the engine, and I stood back to let her pull away. But she rolled down the window and stuck her head out.

"Meet me there. It's the pub on Oden St."

A frown strained at my forehead. I wanted to pick her up. Like a proper date. But for now, I'd let her call the shots.

"By the way, how old are you going to be?"

"Thirty-five."

She let out a low wolf whistle. "Don't worry, old man. I'll remind you how to have a good time." She winked, and it only made me like her more. She had a spark that was damn infectious.

Suddenly, I was looking forward to my first birthday "alone."

10

He was going to stand me up.

The evil, hateful voice in my head had been telling me that for the past week. I'd had my personal session with Beau on Wednesday, which had bolstered my confidence again. He'd mostly been professional, but the air between us had been thick with something unspoken.

On my end, there was no doubt it was lust. I couldn't stop looking at the man. I was so damn attracted to him I was surprised my underwear didn't melt every time he was around. He'd confirmed our Sunday night date, but sometime between Wednesday and right now, I'd convinced myself he wasn't going to show. He was too hot. Too nice. Too *everything* to be interested in me. I knew I was smart and kind of amusing if not actually funny. I was fun, for the most part. But physically, I felt incredibly subpar, and the toned bodies of the women training in the gym hadn't helped that any.

I reminded myself that Beau had been the one to ask me out. Sort of. He'd show.

With shaking fingers, I took a seat at the bar and ordered a drink, trying not to stare at the doors. I was ten minutes early. There was no need to panic yet.

"Hey," a voice said behind me, and I spun to find myself looking up at Beau's rugged features.

"Hey!" I choked out. "Where did you come from?"

"The other end of the bar. I saw you come in."

Oh. He was early too.

I liked that. I hadn't even considered that he might beat me here.

"So," Beau said, his forehead creasing as he took the stool next to mine. "I heard something incredibly disturbing a minute ago."

I toyed with the rim of my beer bottle, feigning ignorance. But I had a good idea where this might be heading.

"Oh?"

"The bartender told me the pub choir would be starting any minute now. Want to fill me in on what a pub choir is, exactly?"

I grinned. "I hope you like to sing."

"Oh, I love to sing. It's the people around me who don't like it."

I giggled and that made him smile. My heart gave a pathetic flip-flop. I was already such a goner.

"You have a great laugh, you know." He leaned on the bar top, his shirt stretching over his pecs.

So distracting. "I sound like a donkey."

That made him double over. And funnily enough, it was *him* who sounded kind of like a donkey. Which only made me laugh all the harder. It was nice to know he wasn't actually perfect.

When I calmed down, I went back to explaining what pub choir was. "So they give you some time to get drunk. But then we all learn a song, and in a few hours, we all sing it together. The whole room."

Beau took a swig of his beer. "You actually came here knowing this is what we'd be doing?"

I nodded, trying to hide my amusement at his appalled face.

"Can you sing?"

"Nope. Not at all."

"So we're both going to suck?"

"You, me, and probably half of the room. It's not about being good. It's about letting go and having fun. You look like you need it."

He put his beer down and twisted it idly on the bar top. "It's been a pretty shitty six months."

I signalled for the bartender to bring us another round before I addressed his comment. "I know we're on a date, but we're kind of friends, right?"

He nodded.

"So, asking purely as a friend, has it been shitty because you miss your wife?" My pathetic, already falling heart squeezed in nervous anticipation of his answer.

He shook his head so quickly it left no room in my mind for doubt. And thank God, because seeing him out of gym clothes was doing all sorts of things to my libido. I wanted to be his friend, sure, but I wanted to be a hell of a lot more than that too.

"I miss my kids. It's really hard going from seeing them every day to once or twice a week."

I reached out and laid my fingers on his arm, rubbing it gently. It was nice that he cared so much about his children. I'd never felt that sort of love from my father. He loved me in his own way. I knew that. But I think he probably wouldn't have minded if he'd only had to see me at training.

Beau stared down at my hand for a moment, and I followed his gaze, noticing how my pale skin contrasted with his deep tan. He covered my hand with his own, and my heart skipped a beat, before the moment was over and we both went back to our drinks.

"It's not just the kids," Beau said, picking up the conversation again. "It's the gym too. You might have noticed how quiet it is."

I shrugged, non-committal, not wanting to make him feel worse, but he saw right through that.

"Yeah, you've noticed. It's hard to compete with TAS." He looked over at me and pasted a smile on his face. It didn't meet his eyes though. "But there's a tournament coming up. If I have fighters who do well in each division, it could really bring us some good publicity. I don't need to be as flashy as TAS. I'm the better trainer. I know that. I just need other people to see it too."

"Are you going to fight?" I asked, not sure whether I wanted his answer to be yes or no. On the one hand, I already cared enough about him to not want him hurt. On the other hand, the thought of him fighting was kind of brutally hot.

"Yeah, for sure. I need to beat the Tanner brothers. With four of them in the same division as me, I'll be up against at least one. It's been over a year since the last time we competed, but if I could take the title..."

"It'd help your business?"

"At this point, it's more about saving it than helping it."

Shit. That sounded dire.

"Actually, I wanted to talk to you about the tournament too. You're my only white belt and I really want to be represented in each category. I know you've only had a few lessons, but you're a natural. And I really think you could do well."

I shook my head hard. "Oh no, no, no."

"Why?"

Because my brothers and my dad will be there? Because you'll realise I'm a part of that family business you hate so much? The one that's sending you out of business?

And because you'll realise I've been lying this entire time.

I sighed. "I'll get my ass kicked, Beau."

"You really won't. You've got natural talent."

Ugh. I had to tell him.

"Beau—"

"Excuse me, everyone!" A woman on the stage said into the microphone, saving me from the world's most awkward conversation. A breath of relief escaped me. My brain whispered accusations, calling me a coward, but I downed my drink. If I had enough of them, that annoying voice in my head might drown. Fingers crossed.

"We're about to get started. We're doing *Prisoner of Society* by The Living End tonight. We'll split the room into sections in a minute, and the words will be projected up here on the wall. Or grab your phone and look up the lyrics there if you want. But this is your last warning. If you need liquid courage, now is the time to grab it." She switched the microphone off, and we all cringed as it squawked through the room.

Beau turned straight to the bartender and ordered four shots of tequila. I raised an eyebrow.

"Don't judge, two are for you."

"Trying to get me drunk?"

"Trying to get us both drunk."

We downed our shots and for the next ninety minutes we drank while the woman on stage taught the entire room full of people how to sing a rock song in three-part harmony. Beau started out barely mumbling the words, but the more we drank, the more we both got into it. The vibe and excitement in the room was infectious, and it was impossible not to get pumped up.

"Right! It's time to do this thing! Group one, stand on this side of the room; group two, here in the middle; group three, over there. Oh, and don't look at the cameras."

A murmur of surprise rippled through the crowd and the

woman in charge laughed. "Did I not mention we're filming this? It'll be up on YouTube by the end of the night."

Beau's fingers slid between mine, and I looked up at him in surprise. Alcohol and excitement thrummed through me, and that only heightened at the feel of his large hand wrapped around mine. My heart thumped. "We're in different groups," I said sadly. The organiser had split most of the men into the baritone group one. I was group two, as a woman who couldn't sing the high notes.

"We'll stand on the line in between. I'm not doing this without you," he said firmly.

He stared down at me, and suddenly, all I could think about doing was kissing him. I wanted to pull his mouth down to meet mine, so this heat building within me had some place to go. I ran my tongue over my lips, capturing his attention, and his hand gripped mine tighter. He pulled me close, my palm hitting his hard chest, and I had to tilt my head back to keep the burning eye contact that held me in place.

My breath caught.

He was going to kiss me.

His eyes shone glassy green, a sure sign he'd been drinking, but they were focused and clear and told me everything I needed to know. He wanted this too. Heat travelled through me like a rocket, stopping between my legs. My breasts tingled at the nearness to him, alcohol making me floaty and brave. Our lips drew closer like some invisible force had control. My eyes shuttered closed of their own accord.

"Okay, let's do this!" The organiser's voice boomed around the room.

The delicious feel of Beau's pecs under my hand disappeared as he stepped back, and I opened my eyes again. Disappointment crushed in on me. I turned away and sought out the organiser on the stage. I'd hunt her down and feed her to Bree's bitchy cat later. Could the woman not see the man of my dreams was about to kiss me? Gah!

But then Beau's fingers squeezed mine, and I tried to school my features into something that wasn't full of the desperation I was feeling.

"Later, sweetheart," he whispered. Then he nodded up to the stage. "Are we going to sing, or what?" He gave me a sly grin.

I stuffed my feelings over my missed opportunity away. There wasn't time for that. Not when we were about to be filmed. And his promise of "later, sweetheart" rebounded around my brain. I cracked my knuckles. I could be patient. "Well, I'm ready to give a stellar performance. But I don't know if I'd call what you've been doing all night singing," I quipped.

The woman at the front of the room counted us in, and for the next four minutes, Beau and I and the two hundred or so people surrounding us belted out that Living End song like we were seasoned rockstars. Beau did all the low bits, my group sang the middle of the range stuff, and by the end of it, we were all jumping up and down and singing like no one was watching.

And it was the most joyful, liberating experience of my life.

Watching Beau let go, while my own inhibitions left my body, was a heady feeling.

At the end of the song the room burst into cheers and applause. I threw my free hand up in the air and cheered along with everyone else, before Beau pulled on the hand that was still linked with his. He spun me to face him and before I could even catch my breath, his lips were slamming down on mine.

Without a second of hesitation, I kissed him back with just as much vigour. His hands found my lower back, and my breasts pushed into his chest as our tongues moved together, desperate and wanting and full of the pent-up sexual tension I'd been feeling all night. My fingers fisted in his shirt and the rest of the room, their cheers and yells, all melted away. All that existed was the feel of Beau around me.

A rough growl came from Beau's chest as he gripped the back of my neck, slanting his head to deepen the kiss, and making my world spin on its axis. We kissed like we'd done it a thousand times before. He was fresh and exciting while somehow still being comfortable and safe. And God, I wanted more. My core throbbed. If we hadn't been in the middle of the pub, I would have ripped his clothes off then and there.

Eventually, I got the sense of the crowd around us moving toward the exits, and we pulled away, our breathing fast.

"Cleo, I..."

Silence fell between us, our breaths mingling in the tiny gap between our bodies.

"You what?" I breathed. *Please say you want to take me home and fuck me senseless,* I prayed. Because that's what I wanted to say. That's what that kiss had been leading to, hadn't it? It sure felt like it.

His mouth dipped to mine again, this time lighter, softer, sweeter.

"We should go."

Through hazy eyes, I dipped my head in agreement. "Okay." Though I was anything but okay after a kiss like that.

"Work tomorrow, you know?"

Right. Work. Work had been the last thing on my mind. But he was right. I tried to step away, scared my disappointment was written all over my face, but his fingers held me in place. I looked up at him questioningly, and I could see him warring with himself.

That bolstered my confidence. "Neither of us can drive. Want to share an Uber?"

Beau groaned and leaned down to rest his forehead against mine. "I can't."

"Why not?" I whispered.

"Because if I get in an Uber with you, I'm not taking you home. I'm taking you back to my place."

Excitement lit up my chest again. "And that would be bad because…"

Beau closed his eyes.

"It's your birthday, Beau."

"You want to be my present?" His words were deep and guttural and had the most pleasant effect on my body.

"If you want me to be."

God, who was I? I was being more forward with a man than I'd ever been in my life. Which left me incredibly vulnerable. But I wanted him. I didn't want to go home alone.

"Are you kidding? Of course, I fucking want you, Cleo," he growled. He pulled me tighter, so our bodies were flush, and I felt the considerable bulge in his jeans that told me exactly how turned on he was. I slipped my hand between us and down over the bulge, making him groan and flex his hips into me just a fraction. But then he stepped away, messing with his shirt to make sure it covered him. "Good things come to those who wait, Cleo. And I want to be a gentleman."

Screw being a gentleman! I wanted to throw myself on the floor and have a toddler-style tantrum.

He led me to the door of the rapidly emptying bar, and outside, he ordered Ubers for us both. When mine arrived, he kissed me sweetly, then held the door open. I pouted out the window, but he just laughed and shook his head.

"See you at training tomorrow."

Tomorrow night couldn't come soon enough.

11

"Camden! Concentrate!"

The look he shot me could have killed. If I hadn't raised the kid to have good manners, he probably would have flipped me off. I could tell he wanted to. But he was pushing my patience. He was moving around the mats like a slug, forcing me to put on my coach hat and nag him to get his head in the game. There was only a handful of days until the tournament, and if he fought the way he was training right now, he'd be laughed right off the mats.

Through the glass panelling, I saw the gym door open and a flash of red hair fly through.

She was here.

I'd been sneaking glances at the door all night, waiting for her. I paused, watching until her gaze found mine, and when she smiled at me, my heart skipped a beat. For the past two weeks, ever since that night where I'd practically ripped her clothes off in the middle of the pub, she'd come to training every night. And I was amazed at the quick progress she'd made. She had a style to her form that most beginners didn't possess, and once we improved her fitness, she'd be something amazing.

There was an untapped potential in her that excited me. She was already good enough to enter tournaments in the beginners' levels. I just had to convince her to do it. But with all the training she was doing, I had a feeling she might come around.

She still did her personal class with me on Wednesdays, though I'd made a habit of finishing early so we could spend the last ten minutes of class making out. But the other days, she'd join in with the group classes or spend time on the cardio equipment. She often hung around until closing, and each night we'd talk as I walked her to her car. But I'd been true to my word.

I wanted to be a gentleman. I wanted to take things slow with her.

We'd developed a nice friendship, and even though the sexual tension between us had me jacking off like a fifteen-year-old finding his cock for the first time, I still hadn't made a move to take things further. Stealing kisses when we should have been training was as physical as I'd let myself get.

But fuck. When she gave me that smile, that special one she seemed to save just for me, it made me forget all promises of gentlemanly behaviour. How long was I supposed to wait? It had been three weeks since we'd met, I had to be getting close. I hadn't dated in so long, I didn't know what the rules were anymore.

"Dad, can we stop? Mum's here."

"You've still got ten minutes."

Camden let out a huff and went back to half-heartedly kicking a freestanding punching bag. His form was sloppy, his kicks weak. He could do better.

I sighed, turning back to Ayva who was cartwheeling around the room instead of running the drills I'd asked her to do. I bit my tongue. I loved my kids more than anything, but sometimes it was hard to be their dad *and* their coach.

Time to give up for the night. I searched the foyer for Cleo again, but she'd disappeared. My ex, Jane, was there though. I called the end of class and ignored the *finally* that Camden mumbled under his breath. He trudged out, while Ayva skipped in circles around him. I put away the equipment we'd been using, and by the time I met them in the foyer, Jane had Camden's face cupped in her hands, talking to him quietly.

She looked up as I approached, then handed him her car keys. "Take Ayva and wait in the car, okay?"

Camden moved toward the door, but I grabbed him and pulled him back to me, kissing the top of his head. "Bye, mate. I love you." Then I picked Ayva up for a hug before I let them go.

Jane had her hands planted firmly on her hips when I turned back to her. I tried not to roll my eyes. I knew that look. I was in for it.

"What have I done now?"

"It's more like what you haven't done," she huffed. "Or more accurately, what you aren't seeing. He hates martial arts, Beau. Can't you see that?"

I shook my head. "*You* hate martial arts, Jane. Don't project onto him."

She threw her hands up in the air. "It's not about me and you! He's miserable. He's only doing it to keep you happy."

I narrowed my eyes. "Did he say that?"

"Well, no, not exactly."

I thought as much. "I'm pushing him hard right now because we have a tournament on the weekend. All kids go through phases of hating their coaches."

"But you aren't just his coach. You're his dad. Do you really think he's capable of separating the two?"

I opened my mouth, but she shook her head and patted me on the arm. "I don't want to fight. Just think about it, okay?"

I ground my teeth together as I watched her walk through the door and disappear into the darkness.

That was bullshit. Wasn't it enough that she already had the kids full-time? The judge in our custody case had awarded me this time with the kids. She couldn't take that away. And making me feel like I was a shit parent, forcing my kid to do something he didn't want to do, was low. I spun and stormed my way down to the personals room, slamming the door behind me. I needed a minute to get myself under control. I sunk down onto one of the benches and leant forward, bracing my elbows on my knees, letting my head drop.

Guilt swirled in my gut. Did he hate it?

No, screw that. She was playing mind games with me again. Just like she had when we were married. She'd made me think it was me who had been the shitty spouse when she'd been cheating all along. I hadn't cared about that, our feelings for each other had been long dead. But this was different. Camden was my son, and I wasn't going to be pushed out of his life.

I launched onto my feet, storming across the small space to where the punching bag hung from the wall.

"Fuck!" I yelled, taking a swing at it.

The door behind me opened and closed, but I couldn't have cared less. I let my confusion and frustration flow through my fists and feet, punching and kicking the bag. I pounded the leather over and over, the thwack of flesh connecting and splitting open the only thing keeping me from completely breaking down. The pain in my knuckles distracted from the pain in my chest that ran much deeper.

I didn't stop until I heard Cleo's voice cut through my fog.

"Beau, stop."

I whirled on her. She took a step back, but when desire flickered in her eyes, I closed the distance between us until I had her pinned against the wall.

Every muscle in my body coiled tight, too tight. I needed

somewhere for all the pent-up energy to go, and the boxing bag wasn't cutting it.

Without another thought, I slammed my lips down on Cleo's. Her gasp told me I'd taken her by surprise, but then her arms snaked around my neck and into my hair and she was kissing me back just as hard. It was suddenly like no time had passed, and we were back in that pub, our mouths finding each other, hungry and wanting. Desperate.

I slid my palms down her curves, over her hips to her ass, loving the way it filled my hands perfectly. I gripped her tightly, hoisting her up, her legs wrapping around me. With only my thin gym shorts and her Lycra pants between us, my cock, already thick and hard from our kiss, rubbed against her pussy.

My lips found her neck and her head dropped back as I sucked the delicate skin, nipping at it with my teeth. We'd gone this far before, kissing until we were out of breath, but desperation for her clawed through me. Kissing wasn't enough.

I flicked the lock on the door with one hand, then held her close, carrying her over to the mats. I set her down in the middle, then checked her expression to make sure she was okay with where this was going. And there in her eyes, I found everything I wanted. Compassion. Lust. Want. Need.

And there was the beginning of something more. Something that startled me, but after my initial surprise, left me warm.

I pushed her hair back off her face and kissed her sweetly, before I found the hem of her shirt, lifting it up and over her head. We both kicked off our shoes and socks, and I reached back to grab my shirt, yanking it off with one hand. Her fingers fumbled with the drawstring on my shorts, and my dick kicked at how eager she was.

I hooked my fingers in the waistband of her leggings and dragged them down her body, before kissing the fuck out of her mouth. She moaned and my balls clenched. I needed her naked faster. I needed her naked now.

Unhooking her sports bra, I freed her breasts and immediately ducked my head to suck on one pink nipple. God, I'd wanted a taste of her skin for so long.

Her head fell back as my hot mouth closed over her tip and I swirled my tongue over the sensitive flesh. I cupped her other breast, teasing and rubbing her nipple until it hardened under my touch. Impatient, I kissed my way down her body, over the curve of her belly, and drew her underwear down her legs, leaving her completely bare. And then I took a long moment to just drink her in.

"Sit on the bench, Cleo," I commanded.

She did as I said, moving to the bench, but covered her belly with her arms. I knelt before her, my knees sinking into the mat.

"Don't do that," I said, pulling her arms away while pushing her knees wide with my shoulders. "Not with me."

She blushed an adorable shade of pink but kept herself covered. I raised an eyebrow at her. Fine. I'd take that as a challenge. If she wanted to play it like that, I'd do other things until she forgot about being self-conscious.

I shifted her to the edge of the bench, my dick throbbing and straining as her pretty pink folds opened to me. I couldn't resist. I leant in and ran my tongue through the centre of her, tasting her sweet flavour and savouring it on my tongue. Her body jerked. I did it again, and again, and smirked when she unwrapped her arms from her middle to lean back on her hands, giving me better access to worship her.

Spurred on, I circled her clit with my tongue, watching in fascination as she abandoned herself to the sensation. Her head dropped back, her back arched, and her amazing tits pressed high to the sky. The sight nearly had me coming all over my shorts.

"You're so beautiful, Cleo," I murmured against her inner thigh. "Don't you ever hide from me again. Not when you look like that."

She didn't reply, but her hips rocked against my mouth, urging me back to my work. And I went willingly, burying my face in her pussy, letting her taste and scent surround me. When she began writhing on the bench, I ran one hand up her inner thigh, finding her wet slit and pushing two fingers up inside her.

"Oh," she cried out.

I didn't care that we were at my gym. Anthony was out at reception and there was a class starting soon, but in that moment, all I could see and think and do was her.

"Lie back, baby," I whispered. "I got you."

She did as I said, collapsing back onto the bench and I hooked her legs over my shoulders, opening her up all the way. My fingers plunged in and out of her tight core, while my tongue lapped at her folds and rolled over her clit.

"Oh God," she moaned. "Beau, I'm going to come."

My dick wanted in on the action so badly. I could feel the precum leaking from my tip, readying me to plunge inside of her, but I forced myself not to move. I wanted to see her come apart first. My fingers moved faster and faster. Over and over I angled them, finding the most sensitive spot up inside her until her moans became cries and her walls clenched down on my fingers.

"Oh! Beau!" she cried as she came, pulsing hard. Her hands gripped my head, holding me, guiding me, pulling away, then anchoring me to the spot as if she wanted more but didn't know if she could take it. I stayed there for a long time, riding out her orgasm with her until I'd wrung out every last drop of her pleasure.

I pushed to my feet and took in the sight of her, splayed out on the bench, every naked, gorgeous inch of her, not a hint of her earlier body shame in sight. And I wanted more.

I yanked the drawstring on my shorts, reaching inside to pull out my aching cock—when three sharp knocks at the door had me freezing with my fingers wrapped around my erection.

Cleo sat up sharply, her head whipping from side to side as she looked for something to cover herself with. I threw her my shirt and stormed to the door. "What!" I barked through it.

Anthony's voice, laced with laughter, came back at me. "Ah, boss? Your class was supposed to start five minutes ago."

I looked at my watch. Had we seriously been in here for forty minutes? I looked back over my shoulder at Cleo scrambling for her clothes.

"Go," she mouthed at me.

I was torn. The last thing I wanted to do was go teach a class. I wanted to go right back to where I'd been a minute ago, about to sink myself into a beautiful woman. But I'd already shirked my Wednesday classes onto Anthony, I couldn't do that again. Especially since his laughter told me he probably knew we weren't training back here. I strode across the room and grasped Cleo by the back of the neck, pressing my lips down on hers. I kissed her hard and fast and when I pulled away, I whispered, "That was the hottest thing I've ever fucking seen, Cleo. And I want to do it again. Tell me I can."

She bit her lip, stifling a smile. "There are some things I want to do, too. Tomorrow?"

"Can't. Training." I groaned. "Actually, I'm training all week."

"Saturday. After the tournament. I don't want to be a distraction."

I ran my finger down the side of her face. "You're a distraction even when you aren't here. Because when you aren't here, I'm still thinking about you."

I moved toward her again, but she held her hand up in a stop motion. "Seriously. Saturday."

I frowned. Saturday was almost a whole week away.

She laughed as if she'd read my mind and pushed me away. "It's only a few days. You need to train. And your fighters need you to coach. Go."

She held out my shirt, and I reluctantly pulled it over my head.

"Saturday night, Cleo."

A wicked grin spread across her face. "We'll celebrate. Martial arts isn't the only thing I'm naturally good at, you know."

I let out a guttural groan. I could only imagine.

12

———

When I crawled into bed, my body was still buzzing from the mind-blowing orgasm I'd had at the gym. It had to be the least sexy place on Earth, but no woman in her right mind was going to turn Beau down when he stripped you naked, laid you out, and went down on you until you saw stars.

I couldn't wipe the grin off my face as I'd driven home. I'd played it over in my head again while I showered, and I knew I'd be reliving it as soon as my eyes closed. I settled back against my pillow, just drifting off when I remembered something.

I reached for my phone on my bedside table and found Beau's number in my messages.

Cleo: *Hey, you still awake?*

His reply came straight back.

Beau: *Just got into bed.*

I couldn't help smiling at that thought. I briefly wondered what he slept in, before deciding he was 100% the type to sleep nude. The thought made me flush hot. But that wasn't why I'd messaged him.

Cleo: *I just wanted to check if you're okay. That's why I came *after you tonight. I saw you arguing with your ex, and you looked upset.*

Beau: *So, you didn't actually follow me for oral sex?*

Cleo: *Ha. Sorry, no. But that was a happy bonus.*

I toyed with the edge of the bedspread, waiting for his reply. The three little dots on the message screen that told me he was typing kept appearing and then disappearing, and I wondered if he was writing and deleting the message over and over.

Beau: *Jane doesn't want Camden doing martial arts anymore. She says I'm making him miserable.*

Shit.

What was I supposed to say to that? It wasn't my place to get involved in their family situation. They knew their kids better than I did.

The only thing I knew was what it was like to be Camden. I sighed.

Cleo: *Do you think she might be right? Is that why you were so upset?*

My finger hovered over the send button while I debated whether I really wanted to ask. I had no idea how he'd take it. He might tell me to mind my own business. Which would have been totally warranted. Things were just getting started with us. I didn't want to ruin them before they'd even had a chance to begin.

But I'd seen the look in that kid's eyes and seen a younger version of myself. I pushed down on the send button before I could analyse my actions any further. The message pinged off into the universe.

I immediately regretted it. But I couldn't take it back. And I couldn't just lay still and watch the phone. The pleasant sleepy feelings from a few minutes ago had been replaced by wired anxiousness. I got up and paced around the room, pouncing on my phone when it pinged with an incoming message.

Beau: *I don't know. I probably push him too hard, but it's only because...*

That sounded too familiar for comfort.

Cleo: *Because you know how good he can be.*

His response back was almost immediate.

Beau: *No! I just miss him. If he stops coming to training, I'll see him two days a fortnight. Two days. That's not enough. He's getting older, I want to be there for him. How am I supposed to do that if I never get to see him?*

My heart broke a little. He was a good dad, there was no doubt about that. I'd never felt that sort of unconditional love from my father.

Cleo: *Maybe you just need to tell him that. As his dad. Not as his coach.*

Beau: *You're probably right. I just need to get through this tournament. I need him for that. And I need you too.*

Cleo: *Argh. I thought we'd agreed I wasn't doing it?*

Beau: *Please, Cleo? I need the publicity. If I can have a fighter win every division, that would really get some buzz going. You're my only beginner. And you're amazing. I wouldn't even suggest it if you weren't ready. But you are. You're a natural.*

I bit my lip. I didn't want to let him down. That was the last thing I wanted. A big part of me was incredibly excited by the idea of fighting again. The last few weeks had really reminded me what I was missing. And tournaments were the ultimate thrill. A crowd of people, adrenaline pumping through you. It was a massive buzz.

But my one big problem with going to a tournament as one of Beau's fighters hadn't changed. My family would all be there.

Beau: *Come on, you know you want to. I promise you'll love it. Then I'll take you home and make you love it some more.*

I sniggered. I wanted to do it. I wanted to help Beau take out every category. The competitive side of me wanted to kick some ass. The womanly side of me wanted him to watch me do it.

Cleo: *What time is beginners?*

Beau: *First up. 9am.*

My dad and brothers didn't train the beginners' classes. They had a staff of young fighters who worked for them, taking the kids and lower levels. Coaching a white belt was of no interest to them. They only had eyes for the big guns. They probably wouldn't even rock up at the tournament before twelve.

I chewed on my bottom lip, thinking it over.

Cleo: *I'll do it.*

Beau: *I really want to kiss you right now.*

Cleo: *Save it for Saturday, mister. We've got a tournament to win. No distractions.*

13

Closing the gym on a Saturday was probably a bad business practice. I would have bet TAS Sports and Fitness were still open. But with me and Anthony both competing in the tournament today, I didn't have much choice. Neither of us fought until later in the afternoon, but I'd always tried to foster a family feel at these events. We all went to support the team. The beginners and kids were no less deserving of an audience to cheer them on than the black belts were.

Ayva, Camden, and I had gotten to the small local stadium early, to help the organisers set up. Jane had arrived not long after, dressed like she was going to a high tea rather than spending the morning sitting in the bleachers. But whatever.

Camden had seemed quiet and distant again this morning, and I'd had to plaster a smile on my face as I realised that Jane was probably right. The way Camden's eyes had dulled as soon as he started pulling on his gear made my heart hurt. Today would be it, then. His last tournament. It was sad, but seeing him so despondent was worse. I refused to let myself think about the fact that I wouldn't get to see him on Wednesday nights anymore. I'd sacrifice that time if it was what he needed. Even if it killed me inside.

"First call for all white belts. White belts, please register at the table," a static-laced voice echoed around the high-ceilinged room.

I scanned the crowd for Cleo and spotted her coming in the door. She was already dressed in her fight gear, but paused uncertainly in the doorway, taking in the mass of people moving in every direction.

Like a magnet pulling me toward her, I dropped the mat I was carrying and stalked across the room.

"Hey."

She tilted her head back and smiled up at me. "Hey, yourself."

My fingers itched to reach out and grip her hips. To pull her close and kiss her hard. I still remembered the way she tasted, and I'd been starving for it all week. Apart from her personal lesson on Wednesday, where she'd been too nervous about the tournament to entertain my advances, I hadn't gotten to see her at all. I'd been swamped with training myself.

I glanced over my shoulder. "I really want to kiss you," I confessed. "But my kids are here. They don't know about us yet."

A smile twitched at her lips. "Us? I didn't realise we were an *us*."

Something that felt suspiciously like a possessive growl began building in my chest. Maybe I hadn't spelled it out, but we were an us. I hadn't had a woman consume my thoughts the way she did in years. Not caring who saw, I grabbed her hand and pulled her around the corner of the doorway and down a hall that was slightly quieter, if not private. That was probably a good thing, because if it had been any more secluded, I probably would have taken her up against the wall.

Hell. I had to stop thinking like that or I wasn't going to make it through the day. Thank God she was coming home with me tonight.

I chanced someone seeing us, and took her face between my hands, dropping a kiss on her mouth. The kiss was hot and hard, branding, yet over before I wanted it to be. "I want us to be a thing, Cleo. Just you and me. Tell me you want it, too." I knew I was pleading, and that it probably wasn't sexy, but I didn't care. It hadn't even crossed my mind that we weren't exclusive. I kept forgetting that things were different now, to how they'd been the last time I dated.

Until that moment, I'd been confident she'd say yes. There was something between us. I knew it, and I knew she felt it too. I'd felt it the night we'd gone to the bar. I'd felt it when I couldn't keep my hands off her at the gym. I felt it right now, as I stared into her blue eyes. She was the sort of woman I could fall in love with all too easily. And despite the bad run I'd had with Jane, falling in love again was something I wanted. I had a lot of love to give. I wasn't made for being alone.

But now, watching indecision flicker on her face, a knot of worry formed in my gut.

"Cleo?"

"I want to say yes. I do. You're such a good man. And God, just look at you. Anyone who turned you down would be an idiot. But—"

"But you're going to turn me down."

"No! I just...I need to tell you something—"

The crackle of the speakers cut her off. "Final call for all white belts. Please report to the table immediately."

I kissed her quickly. "That's you. We can finish this later. But the main thing is, we're together, right?"

A smile crept across her face and it made my heart thump. She nodded.

I felt like fist-pumping the air. But I tried to rein myself in. "Thank you."

"For what?"

"For competing. For saying yes. For getting me out of my funk. I don't know. But go, quick, before you get disqualified. Go kill 'em."

She grinned and hustled over to the registration table. I stared after her as she walked away, marvelling at how someone I hadn't even known a month ago could come to mean so much to me in such a short space of time.

The first matchups were about to begin. Nervous energy thrummed through my veins, making me jumpy, so I took my seat on the bottom row of the bleachers, moving the Reserved for Coaches sign. These seats would fill and empty throughout the day as the various age and weight divisions were carried out.

Anthony wasn't here yet, so I sat down alone and trained my eyes on Cleo. Being a beginner, she was the first from our club to compete. I desperately wanted her to win. I wanted to set the tone for the day and show the rest of these clubs what we were made of. I wanted them to know we were a real threat, from our kids and beginners, right up to the most experienced fighters.

A big hand clapped me on the shoulder and multiple large bodies sat down on either side of me. I didn't even have to look up to know who it was. I schooled my expression into something verging on friendly, though I probably failed miserably, and gave Mick, the head trainer at TAS, a tight smile.

"Mick."

"Beau."

I offered him my hand to shake and he took it.

"Good to see you. You too, fellas." I nodded at each of Mick's four sons in turn. They called out greetings, but then went back to their conversation. Mick seemed more interested in me though. As head coaches of our respective gyms, I was interested in him too. Though I tried not to show it.

"Anthony fighting today?" he asked, with fake casualness.

I ground my teeth. He'd been trying to poach Anthony ever since the kid had arrived here.

I nodded. "Later. In the boxing competition. What about your boys?"

"Jesse is up later. Same division as you, I'd say."

Great. A chance to kick his ass.

I didn't have any beef with Mick's sons other than the usual rivalry that occurred between fighters who had been competing against each other for years. But I enjoyed it, all the same. I knew I could take Jesse. I was ready.

"Looking forward to it."

"You got any beginners entered?" Mick asked, changing the subject.

"Just one. She's good, though. Only been with me a month but has a natural talent I've been impressed by."

"You been training her yourself?"

I nodded.

Mick gave a little laugh and I wanted to roll my eyes. Asshole. I could imagine what he was thinking. That I didn't have enough high-grade fighters to keep me busy. That I couldn't afford to pay someone to train the lower grades like he did. Screw him. Not everyone wanted to run their business the way he did.

"Which one is she? We've got a few in this category too."

I pointed to where Cleo was warming up on the far side of the room. She had her back to us, crouched in a stretch but when she stood and turned, her gaze sought me out. She bounced lightly on her toes, and I gave her a thumbs up.

"No fucking way," Jesse said from behind his old man. "Is that Cleo?"

My head snapped round at the mention of her name. "You know her?"

Mick let out a chuckle from beside me. "We know her. She's my goddamn daughter."

14

The bounce in my step died when I realised Beau was sitting next to my father. And that my brothers occupied the row of seats behind them. Every single one of them stared at me like I'd grown another head. The excitement that had been coursing through me turned to dread.

No, no, no.

Of course, the one tournament I didn't want them to attend, they showed up. Beau looked so confused. I took a few steps toward him, wanting to explain before my father could fill him in, but the official was calling me to the mats. *Shit.* What was I supposed to do? I couldn't just ditch my fight to go running to my boyfriend.

Boyfriend. I hadn't even gotten to say the word out loud.

Hurt flickered over Beau's features, and I turned away. I told myself it was because I needed to concentrate on my opponent, but I just couldn't stand seeing him look at me that way. Up until that moment, his looks had all been filled with admiration. Belief. Lust. He wasn't going to look at me like that anymore, now that he knew who I was. Cleo Tanner. Daughter of his rival. And a big fat liar.

The buzzer sounded and I pushed all thoughts of Beau and my dad out of my head. I couldn't deal with them right now. I'd talk to Beau. Explain everything like I should have the very first day we'd met. The only way I was going to make it up to him in this minute, was to win the match. I threw myself into my kicks and punches. The other woman and I both wore padded vests and head gear, so even though her kicks landed a bunch of times, I didn't feel any pain. Every kick to my chest plate spurred me on. I could feel the pressure of Beau and my father watching me, and adrenaline surged, muscle memory kicking in. I spun, throwing out a spinning heel I hadn't practiced with Beau. It connected and I followed up a series of punches and kicks, forcing my opponent back to the edge of the mats, each blow landing with a satisfying thwacking noise.

Before the buzzer even sounded, I knew I'd won. I let the thrill race through me, turning instinctively to where Beau had been sitting. But his seat was empty. My father's too. My brothers hooted and hollered from the stands, cheering my name, which was kind of sweet. Especially since I wore Beau's logo on my back, while their shirts bore the TAS colours. The people around them must have been so confused, watching my brothers cheer for a rival club, but I smiled when the four of them leaped the barrier and crowded me.

"You were amazing! Why didn't you tell us you were training again?"

I shrugged, pulling off my helmet and pads. "Is Dad pissed?"

Luca shrugged. "He disappeared as soon as the buzzer went."

"What about Beau?" I asked tentatively.

Jesse shrugged.

I shoved my gear at my brother and pushed through the circle they'd made around me. Searching the room, I couldn't see Beau anywhere. But I knew he couldn't have gone too far. Maybe he'd gone back to the hallway.

I broke into a run, exiting the tournament area, and turned down the hall where less than thirty minutes ago, the man of my dreams had made things official with me.

"Beau," I panted, spotting his still form, leaning against the wall.

He looked up.

"Nice win. Told you you'd kill it." But his words didn't hold any joy.

I reached out and threaded my fingers through his, not caring if my dad, my brothers, or his kids saw.

"I'm sorry. I should have told you earlier." I squeezed his fingers.

He looked down at our hands, his face solemn. "Yeah, you really should have. Why didn't you? I still would have trained you."

I sighed. "It wasn't about you, though. It was me. I wanted to do something for myself, without my brothers or my dad finding out. I didn't want to be associated with them. There would have been too much pressure."

Beau was quiet for a moment, the weight of his silence heavy. "You could have done it for yourself without lying," he said eventually.

I hung my head, shame heating my cheeks. He was right. I could have.

"I'm really sorry. I knew how much you hated my dad, and how much rivalry there is between the two of you, and—"

"Cleo, stop. Do you really think I care who your father is? That's not why I'm upset."

It wasn't? He didn't care that I was the daughter of the enemy? "Then why?"

"Attention please," a voice through the speaker announced.

"It has just been brought to our attention that a club has entered a black belt fighter in the beginner's class. As a result, Cleo Tanner from Elite Martial Arts has been disqualified from the competition."

He pulled his hand away and pushed off the wall, walking past me sadly. "That's why."

* * *

I stormed out of the arena, blinking in the bright light. But once my vision cleared, and locked on my father who stood smoking by his car, I saw nothing but red. "How could you!" I yelled across the parking lot, not caring who heard me. "You reported me as a black belt? I was a black belt when I was fifteen years old for Christ's sake, Dad! I haven't trained in over half my life! Do I look like a goddamn black belt? If I tried to compete at that level I'd be in the hospital!"

Dad stubbed out his cigarette on the tarmac, but I wasn't done yelling. "Why couldn't you just let me have this one thing? Does winning really mean more to you than your own daughter being happy? Because that's what I was, Dad. I was happy. For the first time in my life, I had a man who wanted me, just for me. Who didn't hint that I might need to lose a few pounds. Who didn't call me Roly Poly. Who didn't leave me out of family vacations because I was too fat to keep up with everyone else!"

Dad blinked, his mouth opening and closing before he found the words he was trying to say. "I didn't report you, Cleo. One of the officials recognised your name from back in the day. A lot of these people have been judging since you were a kid. They asked me, and I couldn't lie. You're my daughter, and yes, you haven't trained in a long time, but the fact is, those belts are recognised for life. Beau should have known that."

I bit my lip. Beau probably did know that. I just hadn't given him the chance to tell me. Shit. This had all gone so wrong.

My eyes filled with tears. God dammit. I always cried when I was angry. Though they weren't just angry tears this time. They were tears of disappointment, frustration, and sadness. My dad put his arm around me, and though I wanted to be mad at him, it really wasn't his fault. It was mine. My poor decisions that had led here. I rested my head on his chest again. He kissed my hair, and I vaguely remembered standing in this exact pose, in this exact parking lot, years and years ago when I'd been disappointed over losing my matchup.

"I think I owe you an apology, Cleo," Dad murmured into my hair. "It never occurred to me that you hated us calling you Poly. I'd forgotten why we first started calling you that. We'll stop. And your brothers and I didn't plan that vacation as a family event. I booked the cabin for myself to go hiking for a few days, then your brothers found out and invited themselves. I didn't realise you would want to go. But of course, you can. It's only two bedrooms, but you and I can take those, and the boys can all sleep on the floor. It's in the middle of nowhere and there's not much other than hiking to be done, but I really want you to come. I know your brothers do too."

A light wind blew tendrils of hair into my eyes. I shook my head. "It's fine. You were right. It's not my sort of vacation. I hate the outdoors. And hiking especially. I've always felt like an outsider, and when I realised you were all going on holiday without me, it really compounded that. Taekwondo was the one thing that helped me fit in, but once that stopped, this big void opened up between us."

Dad squeezed my shoulders. "I know. I feel it too. I just don't know how to close it. Your mother would be cursing me if she was still alive, you know. For screwing things up the way I have with you. The boys were easy to keep close. We had martial arts in common. Once you stopped, I didn't know how to talk to you."

I sighed. "I don't want it to be like this."

"Me neither."

I wiped my eyes on his shirt. He was trying. I knew that was hard for him and there was no point in holding a grudge. I had never been willing to give up my family, despite our lack of common interests. And I wasn't going to lose them now either by dredging up more old hurts. Especially not when Dad was clearly trying to have a moment. Responding with more anger wasn't going to help us get to a better place. So as always, I relied on my old friend, humour. "You owe me a family trip. Somewhere nice, where I can lay on a beach while you guys climb mountains and get bitten by bugs."

He chuckled. "Deal. And now that you're training again, we'll have more to talk about."

I shook my head. "I think training is over somehow. I got myself disqualified and made Beau look like a cheat."

"You can always come train with me." Dad raised a hopeful eyebrow.

"Not a chance in hell."

Dad huffed out a breath, but when I looked up, he was smiling. "Talk to Beau. Despite all the business rivalry between us, he's a good guy. Pretty sure he isn't going to kick you out."

Dad hadn't seen the look on Beau's face though. He may have never kicked anyone out of his club before, but there was a first time for everything.

15

———————

I was dressed inappropriately for stalking. That was my primary thought as I sneaked across Beau's front lawn in the darkness. My Taekwondo uniform was all white. If anyone had looked out the window, or driven past, I would be lit up like a spotlight. But in my defence, I hadn't come here with the intention of being a peeping tom.

After my heart-to-heart with Dad, I'd hung around the tournament, skulking in the back rows, just so I could watch Beau fight. And fight, he had. Beau oozed control and strength, his technique impeccable. He'd come up against Jesse, but I'd barely noticed my brother on the mats. My gaze had been laser focused on Beau as he'd taken out the gold medal in a display of speed and agility.

Afterwards, he left quietly with his two little ninjas following behind him. That had thrown me. We'd had plans to spend the night together, but maybe after my disqualification, he'd changed his plans and decided to keep them for the night.

Maybe everything between us was so over he didn't want to see me again.

I'd convinced myself to go home and give him some space.

But by 8pm, I was crawling out of my skin with the need to talk to him. I couldn't just let things sit the way they were. I needed to explain myself. And to apologise. I'd made him look bad in front of everyone at that tournament today. I'd made him look like a cheat, even though I'd explained to the officials what had happened, assuring them Beau had no knowledge of who I was or my history.

I'd tried sending him messages from where I'd sat in my car, outside his house, but he hadn't answered. His ute was in the driveway though, so now, I just needed one quick peep in the window to make sure there were no tiny humans running around and we'd be a go.

The front windows of the house had the blinds drawn tight, so I tiptoed around the side. The windows were higher there, though I could see a light spilling from behind the glass. I jumped, trying to see in, but that wasn't getting me anywhere.

His house was obviously only built for stalkers of the tall variety.

I glanced around, my eyes landing on the garbage bins neatly lined up by the fence. If I could just quietly push one beneath the window—

"Cleo?"

I closed my eyes. I wasn't sure whether to be mortified I'd been busted or grateful that I didn't have to climb, and probably fall through, the garbage bin.

I turned to Beau slowly. "Yep, me. Hey."

He dumped the bag of rubbish he was carrying in the bin and folded his arms across his chest. I studied his expression. He didn't look pissed. Uncomfortable? Maybe a bit confused? I could work with uncomfortable and confused. God knows I was those two things often enough.

"What are you doing out here?"

"I wanted to talk to you."

"By my bins?"

"I was looking for the front door," I lied.

Beau squinted through the darkness. Did he have to be so damn attractive when he didn't understand something? It should be illegal. I probably looked like a stunned squirrel while he just got hotter and hotter. The unfairness was cruel.

"The front door is over there. You know, at the *front* of the house?"

I nodded. "Right. Yep. I don't have my contacts in."

Oh my God. What the hell was wrong with me? I didn't even wear contacts! This was our first meeting all over again. Me running my mouth because I didn't know what to do around him. I was certifiably insane and obviously a pathological liar. His presence seemed to turn me into a crazy person. This was ridiculous. "I'm joking. I don't know why I said that. If my eyesight was bad, I'd be rocking an awesome pair of glasses, not shoving little bits of plastic in my eyes."

Beau looked more and more baffled the more I rambled. Not that I could blame him. Even I didn't know what I was talking about.

I sighed. "Can we please talk? Properly? You know, the kind of conversation where I don't just make stuff up to fill uncomfortable silences?"

He nodded. "Yeah. That would be good. Do you want to come in? Because I think the garbage fumes have gone to your head."

I snorted. Then realised he'd made a joke. A joke! Well, that was something! Maybe he didn't completely hate my guts after all. I held onto that scrap of hope as I followed him back to the front of the house and through the door. We passed empty bedrooms, with single beds that obviously belonged to the kids, but when no small bodies came running around corners, I came to the conclusion they weren't here. I suspected he rented, judging by the generic carpets and beige walls. There wasn't much of his personality in the sparsely decorated rooms he led me through. Knowing he'd only separated from his wife six months ago, it made sense that he hadn't yet put in a lot of time to make this place feel like a home.

He gestured to a new-looking lounge, and I perched on the edge uncertainly, hating how we'd gone from stealing kisses this morning and counting down the minutes till we could get naked, to this weird, stilted conversation that was much less enjoyable than being in our birthday suits.

But then he sat down next to me and hope rose. He could have taken a seat at the other end of the lounge. Or on an armchair, well away. But he'd picked the spot right beside me. Even with a few inches separating us, I felt those sparks between us crackle to life again.

I wanted to inch closer, and "accidentally" lean into him, just so I could feel his skin against mine. But my brain was already scrambling just being this close to him. Touching him wasn't going to help that. And I owed the man an explanation. Or three.

I twisted so we faced each other and stared into his deep green eyes, memorising them, in case he kicked me out and I never got to see them this close again. That thought made my heart ache. I didn't want to go back to staring at him through the blinds of the waiting room. That wasn't ever going to be enough. Not anymore. Not after knowing what it felt like to be his friend. To be held in his strong arms. To have my body worshipped in a way no other man ever had.

I was so busy staring at him and becoming overwhelmed with emotion that in the end, he was the first one to speak. "I just want to know one thing, Cleo. Was any of this real? Was this all some ploy to run my club into the ground so your father could buy me out at a cheaper rate?"

I recoiled. "What? No!" I spluttered. "I know my behaviour hasn't exactly warranted trust, but you've got to believe that was never my intention." I stared him hard in the eye. "You don't really think that, do you?" The question came out as barely more than a whisper. The thought too awful to bear.

He threw his hands up in the air. "That's the thing, Cleo. I don't know. You lie a lot. You lied about your name when we first met. You lied about who you were the entire time we were hanging out together. Pretty sure you lied to me just now about not knowing where my front door was."

I cringed. He was right. I slumped back on the lounge, letting the fluffy cushions wrap around my shoulders. "You're right. I swear, I'm not normally like this. I don't lie just for the fun of it. The first lie was because I was flustered, and I wanted to know you. I'd spent so long watching you through a window, completely intrigued by you. I just wanted a reason to be there, in your presence. Then I lied about who I really was, because I wanted training to just be about me. Not who everyone thinks I should be, because of who my dad and brothers are. But not only that, I wanted to keep hanging out with you. I knew there was bad blood between you and my father. I didn't want to risk never seeing you again. I was going to tell you, I swear. I never expected things to get serious with us. I was going to tell you today, before my match, when you asked if we were exclusive. But then there wasn't time."

He shook his head. "Why didn't you tell me you're a black belt? I feel stupid for not realising earlier. Nobody, even those with natural talent, picks up martial arts as quickly as you did."

I cringed. "I didn't realise I was still considered a black belt. I promise, I didn't knowingly lie about that. I got that black belt when I was ten, Beau. And I stopped training at fifteen. It was half my lifetime ago. I had no idea it stayed with you forever. I know how bad all of this looks, but it was completely unintentional."

A little of the tension seeped out of the rigid set of his shoulders. "I might be an idiot, but I believe you."

I stilled. "You do?"

"My gut already told me all of this. I just wanted to hear it from your mouth."

Hope sparked in my chest. "So, does that mean we're okay? We can still be...friends?" I closed my eyes, waiting for his response. If I couldn't have him in my life as my boyfriend, at the very least, I wanted him as a friend. I couldn't stand the thought of seeing him at work every day and never speaking to him. I wanted to keep training as well. He'd rekindled a flame in me, and I wasn't ready for that to be snuffed out just yet.

"Cleo, I can't."

My little flame spluttered and died.

My chest ached. I wished I'd done the whole thing differently. It had taken me so long to find a man worth keeping, and I'd built this whole thing with him on a lie. Was it any surprise the whole thing had fallen down around my ears?

Beau's warm fingers wrapped around mine, and I blinked back the tears threatening to drop on our entwined hands. Ugh. Even when he was breaking up with me, he was the sweetest.

"Cleo, look at me. Is that really what you want? To just be friends? Because I meant what I said today. I want more than that."

My head snapped up. "What? But—"

"But yeah, you fucked up. But I can see why you did it. I was pretty vocal about my distaste for your old man and his gym. I probably wouldn't have mentioned I was the daughter of Satan either."

He grinned, showing me he was joking, but it was the most

beautiful sight in the world. My little flame of hope ignited once more, swirling and becoming an inferno.

"So, you aren't breaking up with me? You're saving me from being in the *Guinness Book of World Records* under the shortest relationship ever?"

He chuckled and moved close enough for his warm breath to mist over my lips. "Well, my name would be right there next to yours, and that *would* be kind of lame."

"What about my family?"

He shrugged. "What about them? I come with baggage too, you know."

"Your baggage is a hell of a lot cuter than mine, though."

"True," he agreed. "Your brothers are on the pretty side, but I think Ayva has them beat."

I smiled, but it was hard to keep it there. "Seriously, though. My dad is still going to want to buy out your business. He won't stop just because we're together."

Beau shrugged and leant in, making me shiver. His eyes dipped to my lips, and my heart skipped a beat. My skin tingled at his nearness. His mouth hovered over mine, and my eyes fluttered closed. "Cleo," he murmured. "Can we stop talking about your dad and my kids? We can worry about that later. Isn't this the part where we kiss and make up?"

I made an affirmative noise from deep in my throat, too caught up in my attraction to him to form real words. He was right. We had plenty of time to work out the details, and there was nothing I wanted more than to stop talking and just enjoy my time with the man I'd almost let slip through my fingers.

"Thank God, because I've been wanting to do this all week."

Beau's lips met mine, and it was soft and sweet and so tender it made my heart ache. He pulled me onto his lap as our lips moved together, and I straddled his legs, my knees pressing into the soft lounge cushions on either side of him.

"You have?" I whispered against his mouth. "Because I've been waiting to do this."

I lifted the hem of his shirt and fought the urge to sing a hymn of praise as his perfectly sculpted body was revealed. I pushed to my feet and almost laughed at the way his face fell as I moved away from him. But his expression changed when I pulled him up with me. Finding the waistband on his pants, I slid them down his legs, taking his underwear with me. Then knelt at his feet to pull them off. When he was bare, I ran my palms up his calves and the muscled planes of his thighs, over the light dusting of hair on his skin. Then looked up at him as his cock, already thick and hard, bobbed in front of my face.

A slight tremor ran through him. "I've been thinking about you looking up at me like that for weeks."

Heat shot straight to my core. The thought of him thinking about me, wanting me, sent warmth across my skin. Without hesitation, I wrapped my lips around the head of his erection. I'd thought about him too. What he'd feel like. What he'd taste like. What it would be like to feel the thick length of him inside me, and feel his body pressed against mine.

Wetness pooled between my thighs as I sucked him. I ran my tongue down his length, then back up, circling the head before taking more. Each time, I took more and more of him, my head bobbing, my tongue and throat working to take in as much of him as I could, that heat between my legs only increasing as his hand landed lightly in my hair.

"God, you're beautiful like that, Cleo. So fucking hot."

His praise only spurred me on. I gripped his heavy balls with one hand, using the other to stroke his length while I sucked on the head. I was all over his erection, touching him in as many places as I could, getting off on the groans he made and the way his fingers fisted and flexed in my hair.

His balls tightened and I renewed my efforts with vigour, but he pushed me away, his breaths coming in short pants. "Stop, Cleo. Christ. I'm going to come straight down your throat if you keep that up."

I looked up at him and gave him a smile that clearly said I wouldn't have minded, and he groaned again. I reached for him, but he pulled me to my feet.

"Not yet," he whispered. His lips brushed the sensitive spot beneath my ear, and he pulled my shirt over my head. My bra followed, and he ducked his head to suck one nipple into his mouth. His tongue rasped over me, and though it felt like heaven, I was impatient for more. Tiny, needy sounds escaped my throat, and if I hadn't already been so turned on from sucking him off, I would have been embarrassed. But without asking, he seemed to know what I needed. He moved down my body, kneeling at my feet, like I'd done to him, and stripped me bare.

He wrapped his arms around my thighs, his fingers gripping my ass as he kissed his way down my stomach. And for the first time ever with a man, I didn't feel self-conscious. I didn't care that I was on display, in a fully lit room with his mouth trailing kisses over my not-flat stomach. I was so hot and achy for him to get between my thighs that the fact that I had a few belly rolls and stretchmarks was the least of my concerns. The only thing I was concerned with was getting him where I wanted him faster.

"Beau," I moaned as he reached the top of my mound. I tried to widen my legs, but he held me tight in his grip.

"I know, baby. I got you. I know what you need."

He kissed over my triangle of short hair, and I whimpered as his tongue pressed between my folds, finding my clit. He finally loosened his grip on me, letting me spread my legs for him, and I was rewarded with one long, hot slick of his tongue straight through my centre.

I nearly came undone right there and then. But Beau was

determined to take his time. He brought me to the edge of orgasm time and time again, alternating between sucking my clit and plunging his tongue through my folds. I clutched his shoulders when my legs began to shake, digging my fingers into his skin to keep myself from melting into a puddle.

"Please, Beau," I moaned.

He chuckled, the vibrations only heightening my need to come. "Is this how you pictured it?" he murmured.

I barely heard him through my haze of lust. "What?"

"Is this how you pictured it when you were stalking me through your office window?"

I slapped his shoulder in mock outrage, and we both laughed. But then his tongue was back, hot and wet, tracing patterns over my most sensitive place. And my laughter was replaced by a needy whimpering.

Right when I thought I couldn't take his torture another minute, there was a crinkle of a condom wrapper, and he stood, lifting me, hooking his arms beneath my knees. I wrapped my arms around his neck, using my thighs to grip his hips. With three long strides, he had my back pressed to the wall.

Then his cock plunged deep within me. I yelled his name, and somewhere in the back of my mind, I heard him yell mine. That was all it took for me to come apart. I came hard, clenching around him and yelling his name again, loud enough that the neighbours probably heard. He'd denied me my orgasm for so long, but there was no stopping it once he was inside me, stretching me wide.

I didn't care who heard us. The orgasm that ripped through me was nothing like any I'd had before. He'd taken his time with me, even when I wanted it fast and hard, and now I was reaping the benefits.

God, he felt amazing. So thick and full as he pushed inside me with each thrust, and I bounced on his dick, riding out my orgasm. He dropped one leg so I could stand, then used his free hand to find my nipple. Another orgasm began to build so quickly it took me by surprise. I'd never quite believed in multiple orgasms, but Beau seemed determined to wring out every last drop of pleasure.

"You with me?" he whispered into my ear, and I moaned my assent. Heat swirled, the now familiar ache opening up again, only to be filled by Beau's cock slamming into my depths. He dropped his hand to my bud, and I cried out as my pussy began to pulse around him for the second time.

"Oh God," I moaned. "Yes!"

Beau groaned as he found his release too, the noise deep, guttural, and oh-so sexy in my ear. He stroked in and out of my core until I was so sensitive I thought I'd never recover. His abs contracted and released as he came within me, a fine layer of sweat making his skin glisten in the lamplight.

When we both stilled, he pressed his chest against mine and found my lips with his own, kissing me sweetly. I barely noticed him pick me back up and carry me to the bathroom.

He turned the shower on, taking a few moments to make sure the spray was the perfect temperature. Then spent the next forty minutes showing me the true meaning of multiple orgasms.

EPILOGUE

One month later...

"As much as I love having your tits pressed into my back, are you sure I can't just close my eyes myself? We're both going down hard if I fall, you know."

Cleo, who I was carrying piggyback style, giggled in my ear, before straining to kiss my cheek. She'd insisted that she get up on my back so she could cover my eyes until we got to the surprise she'd planned for me. She was so much shorter than me, she couldn't hold her hands there properly from the ground, without me crouching.

But now I was stumbling through the darkness, one arm out Frankenstein style, hoping like hell I didn't trip and kill us both.

"Door!" Cleo yelped as my palm hit something solid.

If I could have, I would have rolled my eyes. "Thanks for the warning, babe."

"Sorry. Push."

I did as commanded.

"Do you know where we are?"

Of course, I did. I'd been driving the same route to work

every day for years. I'd pushed open that same door every morning. I knew exactly how it squeaked.

"The gym."

I could practically hear Cleo pouting. "Damn. I didn't think you'd realise if I drove us here."

I chuckled.

"Keep going a few steps, then I'll let you go."

Nervous excitement built in my chest. When Cleo had snuck off out of bed early this morning and told me to sleep in, I hadn't thought much of it, figuring she'd gone to grab us breakfast or something. But when I'd woken up an hour later, still alone, I'd gotten worried. The kids were with us this weekend, but they'd disappeared too. A note on the table, telling me they had a surprise and they'd be back later to pick me up, had left me curious, but at least I'd stopped worrying. Cleo had met the kids almost as soon as we'd made things official, and there hadn't been a single hiccup. They both loved her. And I couldn't blame them. She was great with them. She and Camden had bonded instantly. She'd told him all about how her father had once been her coach too and that had really gotten his attention.

I'd let Camden give up Taekwondo. That had been hard for me, but I'd seen a change in his personality almost instantly. After a week or two of beating myself up over being so blind, I'd chalked it up to one of the many parenting mistakes I'd made, and probably would continue to make, and moved on. I missed having him at the gym on Wednesdays, but Ayva kept me on my toes. And Camden and I made up for it when we did see each other.

"Okay, stop!" Cleo called. A chatter of voices surrounded me, so I knew we weren't alone.

"You ready?" she whispered.

I nodded.

Her hands disappeared from over my eyes, and it took them a second to adjust. But when they did, my mouth dropped open.

"Do you like it?" Cleo asked, as she slid off my back. Her voice was full of worry. But I had no idea why.

"Surprise, Dad!" Ayva yelled, running forward and hugging me round the legs. I dropped a hand to her head as Camden stepped forward, a paintbrush in his hand, his face as uncertain as Cleo's voice had been.

His shirt was splattered with paint, as was Ayva's and Cleo's. That explained why she hadn't let me see her once she'd come to pick me up.

"We're painting," Cleo said.

A grin spread across my face. "I noticed. But this is a bit more than painting." The beginnings of a wall mural were outlined on the back wall of the main training room. My logo, floor to ceiling, in bright blues and greens as well as black. It wasn't finished, but they'd made an amazing start.

"Did you do this?" I asked Cleo.

"Oh hell no. I commissioned it. So if you hate it, it was all my idea."

"I don't hate it. It looks amazing."

"I think so, too. Camden did it."

My eyes widened as I took in my son. "Seriously?"

He smiled proudly. "Cleo bought all the paint. She said she'd pay me to do every room of the gym. It desperately needs a makeover."

"Hey!" I whined, pretending to be hurt.

Cleo nudged me with her elbow. "You know it did."

She was right. And I was crap at the decorating stuff. I knew sports, not paint colours.

Camden and Ayva wandered back to the paint, and Cleo pulled me aside. "I know I'm overstepping, but I thought it could be something that Camden can do here, while Ayva is in class?

So you'd still get to see him during the week?" Her expression was uncertain, like she was worried about my reaction.

"And you think I'm going to be upset by all this?" I pulled her into my arms and felt her body relax a little.

"I don't know. We haven't been together that long, but I know you're missing having Camden here on Wednesdays. And this place definitely needed a paint job. He's an awesome artist, so it seemed like the obvious solution."

I dropped a kiss on her upturned mouth. "It is. You did good."

"I did?"

"Mmmm hmm. I love you, Cleo," I whispered in her ear. My heart raced at the words I hadn't planned on saying. It was the first time I'd admitted that to her, though I'd been feeling it for awhile. Things had been so good between us, and everything within me wanted to hear her say it back. I didn't know what I'd do if she didn't.

She beamed at me, her smile from ear to ear. "I love you, too."

I swept her off her feet, planting a kiss on her mouth. "No lie?" I asked, grinning at her cheekily so she'd know I was joking. It had become a thing with us. Me ribbing her about lying. But she'd promised me no more lies, and she'd kept her word. But I couldn't resist teasing her about it. Normally she just groaned and punched me in the arm. But this time, she looked me dead in the eye.

"I love you, Beau. No lie."

HE END

Here's a sneak peek from book 1, Only the Positive.

"Reese, stop! I have HIV."

The words exploded from his lips like a cannon blast,

halting me in my tracks. The silence was deafening as I slowly turned around.

"What?" I honestly wasn't sure I'd heard him correctly.

He shook his head, one hand gripping the back of his neck. He took a step towards me. "There's a chance I have HIV. A good chance. I've had direct exposure and I'm being tested for it."

My hand flew to my mouth as my heart skipped a beat. HIV? As in AIDS?

He grimaced, his features twisting, his hurt clearly evident on his face. "And that's why I didn't want to tell anyone. I didn't want to see that look of disgust. Especially not from you."

I dropped my hand, shame creeping over me. I wasn't disgusted, but shock rolled through me like a wave, making my movements sluggish. How was I supposed to react?

"Don't worry, you can't catch it from kissing, or from anything else we've done. You're safe."

All the heat and passion between us had disappeared, and where moments before his voice had been sweet, he now sounded sharp and sarcastic. He shook his head and jogged over to his horse.

My feet were rooted to the spot. I wasn't responding the right way. I didn't need his body language to confirm that. But my brain seemed to be disconnected from my body. I had no idea how to make it move, or make it talk. No idea how to make it do anything that would salvage this situation, so we could go back to making out. I touched my fingertips to my lips.

His face was blank when he turned back to face me.

"You see now why we had to stop? I told you it had nothing to do with you. Do you believe me now? I couldn't stay away from you. So maybe you could do me a favour and stay away from me."

Start the series here!

ALSO BY ELLE THORPE

The Only You series (complete)

*Only the Positive (Only You, #1) - Reese and Low.

*Only the Perfect (Only You, #2) - Jamison.

*Only the Truth - (Only You, bonus novella) - Bree.

*Only the Lies - (FREE Only You, bonus novella) - Cleo.

*Only the Negatives (Only You, #3) - Gemma.

*Only the Beginning (Only You, #4) - Bianca and Riley.

*Only You boxset

Dirty Cowboy series (complete)

*Talk Dirty, Cowboy (Dirty Cowboy, #1)

*Ride Dirty, Cowboy (Dirty Cowboy, #2)

*Sexy Dirty Cowboy (Dirty Cowboy, #3)

*25 Reasons to Hate Christmas and Cowboys (a Dirty Cowboy bonus novella, set before Talk Dirty, Cowboy but can be read as a standalone, holiday romance)

Buck Cowboys series (Spin off from the Dirty Cowboy series)

*Buck Cowboys (Buck Cowboys, #1)

*Buck You! (Buck Cowboys, #2)

Saint View High series (Reverse Harem, Bully Romance)

*Devious Little Liars (Saint View High, #1)

*Dangerous Little Secrets (Saint View High, #2)

*Twisted Little Truths (Saint View High, #3)

Saint View Prison - (Reverse Harem, Romantic Suspense)

Book 1: Locked Up Liars (Saint View Prison, #1)

Book 2: Solitary Sinners (Saint View Prison, #2)

Book 3: Fatal Felons (Saint View Prison, #3)

Add your email address here to be the first to know when new books are available!

www.ellethorpe.com/newsletter

Join Elle Thorpe's readers group on Facebook!

www.facebook.com/groups/ellethorpesdramallamas

ABOUT THE AUTHOR

Elle Thorpe lives on the sunny east coast of Australia. When she's not writing stories full of kissing, she's a wife and mummy to three tiny humans. She's also official ball thrower to one slobbery dog named Rollo. Yes, she named a female dog after a dirty hot character on Vikings. Don't judge her. Elle is a complete and utter fangirl at heart, obsessing over The Walking Dead and Outlander to an unhealthy degree. But she wouldn't change a thing.

You can find her on Facebook or Instagram(@ellethorpebooks or hit the links below!) or at her website www.ellethorpe.com. If you love Elle's work, please consider joining her Facebook fan group, Elle Thorpe's Drama Llamas or joining her newsletter here. www.ellethorpe.com/newsletter

facebook.com/ellethorpebooks

instagram.com/ellethorpebooks

goodreads.com/ellethorpe

pinterest.com/ellethorpebooks